The Selected Works of Mahasweta Devi

Mahasweta Devi (b. 1926) is one of our foremost literary personalities, a prolific and best-selling author in Bengali of short fiction and novels; a deeply political social activist who has been working with and for tribals and marginalized communities like the landless labourers of eastern India for years; the editor of a quarterly, *Bortika*, in which the tribals and marginalized peoples themselves document grassroot-level issues and trends; and a socio-political commentator whose articles have appeared regularly in the *Economic and Political Weekly*, *Frontier* and other journals.

Mahasweta Devi has made important contributions to literary and cultural studies in this country. Her empirical research into oral history as it lives in the cultures and memories of tribal communities was a first of its kind. Her powerful, haunting tales of exploitation and struggle have been seen as rich sites of feminist discourse by leading scholars. Her innovative use of language has expanded the conventional borders of Bengali literary expression. Standing as she does at the intersection of vital contemporary questions of politics, gender and class, she is a significant figure in the field of socially committed literature.

Recognizing this, we have conceived a publishing programme which encompasses a representational look at the complete Mahasweta: her novels, her short fiction, her children's stories, her plays, her activist prose writings. The series is an attempt to introduce her impressive body of work to a readership beyond Bengal; it is also an overdue recognition of the importance of her contribution to the literary and cultural history of our country.

OLD WOMEN

Statue
The Fairy Tale of Mohanpur

MAHASWETA DEVI

Translated and introduced by
GAYATRI CHAKRAVORTY SPIVAK

CALCUTTA LONDON NEW YORK

First printing 1997
Second printing 2002
Third printing 2008
This edition 2014

Seagull Books, 2014

ISBN 978 8 1 7046 144 9

Translation © Gayatri Chakravorty Spivak 1999
This compilation © Seagull Books, 1999

'Murti' and 'Mohanpurer Rupkatha' first appeared in *Murti*
(Nabapatra Publishers: Calcutta, 1979)

British Library Cataloguing-in-Publication Data
A catalogue record for this book is available from the British Library.

Typeset by Seagull Books, Calcutta, India
Printed and bound by Hyam Enterprises, Calcutta, India

CONTENTS

Statue

THE DECISION TO RAISE A BRONZE STATUE of Dindayal Thakur, the Freedom Fighter, in Chhatim village, and to dedicate-unveil it with enough pomp and circumstance, and soon, was taken at Calcutta Secretariat, and the announcement appeared in every newspaper. Naturally, the people of Chhatim village didn't know this. The village is *far from the madding crowd*, situated on the outskirts of a state forest area. Soil type *laterite*. Low-yielding. So this soil can't rear and raise a large farming population. The population of Chhatim and seven similar villages is less than 3,000 all total. Government-quota Scheduled Tribes—for example, Santhal–Munda–Bhumij—and similarly Scheduled Castes—for example, Bhunya[1]–Harhi–Muchi–Shunri–Bauri—this is the population. There are not 30 literate persons in the eight villages. The literate are as occupied with filling their bellies as the illiterate. Nobody takes or reads a paper. The nearest police station is 11 miles away. The district town is

1 Caste; also surname.

seven miles away. There you have the necessary *parapher-nalia* such as a *Block*[2] *Development Office*, a *post office*, Forest *Office*, a *social worker training office*, a *school*, the *office of the Sub-Inspector of Schools*, a *health centre*, a grain-storage or agricultural loan realization centre, etc.

The movie theatre is seasonal. Madan Khan of this town (now residing in the firmament) was a fidgety busy-body kind of man. He was two-generations rich in the shellac business. Malicious people say that Madan's dad Badan Khan had received a disproportionate amount of money from the British for helping them capture terror-ist Dinu Thakur, and had invested it in shellac farming forthwith. That money doubled in Madan's hands. For unknown reasons the post-1947 government figured Madan for a patriot and deluged him with *licence permits* as a reward for his service to the nation: licences and per-mits for everything from liquor to bus services. Being rewarded for service to a nation he hadn't served, Madan realized the fruits of having garlanded the picture of Phalahari Baba[3] with wreaths of mangoes–apples–bananas threaded together with a cobbler's needle. Then, for some reason, he becomes desirous of making himself immortal and, driven by said desire, he starts doing many things that benefit the townspeople. Still alive, he con-structs a Madan *Memorial Boys' School*, a Madan Memorial Girls' Learning Centre, a Madan Khan football field, a six-bed Madan Khan hospital, etc., and inaugu-rates them by garlanding his own pictures himself. Finally, the culturalist boys of the town yell 'great national leader'

2 Rural administrative unit, under the District Subdivision.
3 Literally, 'Fruit-eating Baba'. In this case, the name of a 'holy man' or 'guru'.

at him and ask him for a Tagore Institute. Madan Khan
agrees tentatively. But when the Hall is half-finished he
says, My name absent from a hall built from my own
money? It will be Madan–Tagore Hall.

At this stage others enter the fray and explain the
unreasonableness of putting the name 'Madan Khan'
ahead of the name of Rabindranath Tagore. Madan says,
My word is firm. Okay, let it be Tagore–Madan Hall.

As soon as the tin roof goes on the *Hall* his view
changes and he makes his instant decision known. There
is plenty in the name of Tagore, he says. I've decided the
Hall will be in my name after all. And you know what? I
have ordered my statue to be built. I will inaugurate it
myself on Baishakh 25th of 1961, Tagore's centenary.

However *remote*, the place is in West Bengal. The
town's inhabitants are utterly dumbfounded. When they
try to explain how it will be if a Madan Khan Hall is
inaugurated by the living Madan Khan's own hand on
Tagore's centenary, they get yelled at in turn and Madan
says, If you go on like this, I'll make the Hall a paddy
warehouse. This wish of his is not fulfilled, however. For
suddenly he is *transferred* to the firmament by *meningitis*.
The said *Hall* is Tagore *Hall*. It is also the seasonal movie
theatre. For when after harvest the farmer has money in
his pocket, films are shown. At other times all the com-
mittee meetings, all the cultural functions like folk theatre, are held in that *Hall*.

When this is the state of the town, to hope that any
one in Chhatim village would read the newspapers or
know the news was unreal. A vain hope, like seeing *motion*
in a Bengali *motion picture*. So Chhatim dwellers don't get
to know that a statue of Dindayal Thakur, of the vanished
Thakur clan, is about to be established and inaugurated.

At the moment the Thakur compound in Chhatim village is government property. The reason is Dindayal. In 1924, Dindayal was caught, imprisoned, tortured and finally killed on the gallows for the attempted robbery and looting of a train. Consequently, the police subjected his parents, brothers and sisters to unspeakable harassment and confiscated their home and land. The people of Chhatim have no idea that the father-in-law of that very sister of Dindayal, who was two years old at the time of his death, is getting a monthly allowance from the state as his only living relative.

In fact, Chhatimians have almost forgotten that Chhatim village ever had anything to do with Dindayal Thakur. Their days pass in the difficult struggle of share-cropping rice in *laterite* soil, in the casual labour of *felling* Sal trees in forest areas, and as field hands now and then in the fields of Madan Khan's son Sadan Khan. In their gloomy and isolated destitute village there are no services. No *health centre* nearby, no well with water in the village, not even a market, a roadway. You wouldn't know, looking at the village, that there was an arrogant highway just seven miles away. Kharagpur Railway Station is 40 miles away. Undulating land all around, low hills, forests of dwarf Sal, unrelieved poverty. There's a market on Mondays and Fridays at a four-mile distance. A market of salt and pepper, rice and coarse cloth, village-weave towels, eczema ointment and toothache medicine, plastic toys, oil-fried samosas and fried molasses candy.

If an old man has cataracts in a village like Chhatim, or if a man in late-middle age gets short-sighted, they come to the market. Tufan Mollah, with nickel-framed wire-rims of his own manufacture on his nose, makes them for others for four rupees. Suren Hati removes cataracts with lotus thorns or hedgehog spines. Sometimes government functionaries come to the market and shout out speeches about family planning on the megaphone and distribute free and official *literature* on the aforementioned topic in Bengali, in Hindi and in English. The illiterate marketeers rush for the books and the papers. Sell the stuff off to the grocer. If they find a picture they stick it on the wall of their home. Their idea is that the picture of the official happy family with father –mother–son–daughter is actually a picture of the former prime minister of India, her husband and children. This shows how much in the dark they are. They don't even know that lady's *family-structure*—so ignorant.

Not everyone in Chhatim village knows that Dindayal Thakur was actually a freedom fighter. Yes, the Thakur family seat is here. There's a well in the grounds, with water in March and April. But no one takes that water. Impenetrable jungle all around. There's a python there. It's eaten a few goats. No one kills the snake. Why? The Thakurs told the snake to guard their property when they left.

In fact, the people of Chhatim village have forgotten they were always poor. In many of their ever-dark souls the reason for the eternal darkness in their village has come to be the disaster in the Thakur household. The Thakurs departed and Dindayal was hanged in 1924. But this event of 54 years ago lives in their mind as part of the other folk tales, as myth. There are different *versions*, of course.

There's the *version* of the old Santhal aboriginal boat-man Dasu Soren. Many moons ago the Karnabati River flowed here. There was a Bhunya king here. The king had neither son nor daughter. And beggars did not take alms because the king was barren. So the king was sad. He said to his queen, Come let's drown and die in the waters of the Karnabati. Husband and wife leave their kingdom and walk to die by drowning, but the road doesn't end. The queen says, Look. This must be a divine illusion. I see the river from the rooftop every day, bathe in the river on feast days and fast days, it doesn't seem so far! The king is also surprised. Suddenly they see an amazing goddess. Snake-ornaments on her body, snake-crown on her head, standing in air above ground. The king and queen immediately bow down. The goddess says, I am the snake-goddess Manosha. Don't kill yourselves, go back home. You'll have a son. Build a shrine to me here. Let everyone leave a dedicated pitcher for me on the last day of the month of Sraban, let all families worship me. And you must offer me a service everyday, keeping a brahman priest. The king says, Ma, a forest kingdom, a wild king. Where shall I get a brahman? Manosha says, Send a man to the north in the morning. If you walk due north for three hours, you'll see a poor brahman sleeping under a Banyan tree with his wife and children. His fate was bad so far, now by my grace his lot will change. Let the brahman live well and find his feet. Then give him as much land as he can walk in a day in your kingdom. His situation will improve and yours will get better rather than worse. Pay your respects to the brahman, he's not just any old brahman, he's from the Holy City of Varanasi. Dindayal Thakur was a son of that brahman family. The Bhunyas have lost their kingdom and become a farming family, and the Thakurs have left their village.

This folk tale is not supposed to come from a non-Hindu aboriginal. But it was indeed Dasu Soren who told the story. Almost everything in his story is supernatural.

From it a reasonable explanation for the sudden attention of the Calcutta powers-that-be towards Dindayal Thakur's bronze statue cannot be deduced.

Barber Ratan Das's *version* is as follows: Karnabati is long mud-choked. There is a sword and a charter given by someone in the Bhunya house. We have always seen Sadananda Bhunya as a well-to-do farmer. But there's nothing after the land *ceiling*[4] fixed by the government. Now they too buy paddy four months a year. Yes, the Thakurs were their priests. Their house worshipped Manosha. When they left the village Sadananda's father Mahananda asked them to take the image, and this too I've heard from my father, that he wanted to make a monthly allowance to keep up the service. But Thakur's father said, What did I get serving your goddess? I'll say excuse me and leave from here. Then Mahananda Bhunya said, Not a three-a-penny goddess, this is Ma Manosha. Men must live with snakes, you a brahman will offend her? And Thakur said, I'm her priest, yet the police enters my life, my son hanged, evicted from my land, the police touch the body of my women. Worse than this? Let it be. Let mother goddess send a snake and end my line. I have nothing more to do with you. You know what this was? A fight between priest and helper. No, that tiff ended right off. When Dindayal died, this Sadananda was eight. Sadananda is 60-plus, you can't tell. He's eaten well, lived well. His body has that well-fed shine. Sadananda is a feisty type. But his son, Nabin, a good kid. We'll send him to the Panchayat. Chhatim is a bad-luck village. The state forgets that there's a dump called

4 Rural land ownership limits established by the West Bengal goverment as land reforms.

Chhatim. Our Nabin is in *Class Eight*. He goes to the district *town*, gives in our applications and pleas. That's how we got our seed-loan this year. He's trying to pull the paved road from the village all the way to the bus route. For our seven-cursed godforsaken villages there'll be a *health centre* in Chhatim. A rice-loan, farm-loan *centre*, right here. A lot of cash. Work worth 50–60–70 thousand rupees. Good boy, he runs, he runs. I know it won't be. Our village will remain like this. I didn't see, my father didn't, my grandpa didn't see when the village was nice. The village declined when Thakur and Bhunya differed at the hanging of Dindayal Thakur? No no no. A—lways decline, Sir. I run a barber-shop on market days, I even go to Kharagpur, see some more village places, how the village of Temukhi did change! *MLA's* village. Member of the Legislative Assembly! But that *MLA* is an asshole, he doesn't look after us. If anyone says the village was nice, and it fell because of Dinu Thakur, it'll be Sadananda Bhunya. Why they broke, I cannot say. How small we were then?!

Even Ratan Das's version doesn't solve the mystery of the administration's sudden focus on Dindayal Thakur.

Sadananda Bhunya's *version* is *twisted* and full of humbug. Just what happens if you've the name 'Palm Lake' but not enough water to dip a mug in.[5] He points at four adobe rooms, two silos, three plough-steers and a super-strained budget and says, Once my forefathers owned as far as you can see. You might know Mansingh's name, in his time my forefather helped the Minister, and the Minister gave him the title of king. Much much

5 A proverb which means: a grand name without the means to support it.

more. The sword's there, we hear the handle was gold-
plated, we didn't see that. There's a charter, illegible. Of
course we're kings, but now we're in the ditch, no use
talking. My boy loses his temper. Says, So we were kings,
we were kings, that's why such punishment. King of six
acres and a single harvest! He's hot-blooded. A twisted
mind. He ploughs with sharecroppers, my boy. Hasn't
married yet. Says, no income, I'll increase expenses? The
next one is normal. Doesn't work with his hands, has a
wife and two children. Work? What work will he do, with
a Class *V* education? Now he has our household goddess
worshipped monthly, after the priests went we offer the
daily milk–banana–oil lamp–flower ourselves, that
youngest boy gets the monthly rites done by a priest he
fetches from Patke village on his bicycle. The eldest son
has no taste for this side of things. He is most pig-head-
ed. He'll carry a low-caste corpse to the pyre. How does
the younger son support himself? Why? Don't we have
the Manosha fair? We get a cut on all the geese and goats
sacrificed that day, the fair lasts a fortnight, there are earn-
ings there too. Why are we so badly off today, although
we were kings? Because of Dinu Thakur. We lived in
style. The Thakurs were our priests, yes. But they, too,
were given 20 acres of land. Now the Thakur house is
dense jungle. I have seen with my own eyes a lo—ng two-
storey, four-roomed adobe house. The soil here turns to
pumice when it dries with sun in it. It lasts and lasts.
Drawn verandah, a row of rooms. Barns on the other side
of the courtyard. Kitchen quarters, open tank, now all
dry as dust. Huge paved well. Cowshed, and a fence all
around the house. Flower-garden, a guava–papaya–custard apple orchard at the back, their own established god
Radhagobinda, how their shrine-house did glow!

Everything was to our credit. Did they keep that dignity? Everyone knows after all—there's even a book printed, price 12 annas, I myself sell it—everyone knows, Mother Manosha told my forefathers and had them brought to Chhatim. They were poor beggars. Did they pay mind? My pa said, Please my lord, I beg you my lord, and still they didn't take the god? Did they take their own Radhagobinda? Does a priest ever leave his god? (When the story gets to here Sadananda is extremely troubled and wipes the back of his neck repeatedly.) Then Father went to Patke. New arrangements were made after penance with new priests, and begging Mother's forgiveness. In the goddess-clan Mother Manosha takes ferocious form. By her curse the Thakur family went to rack and ruin, and our farm-hand also died of snake-bite. And then look in the village—how the police harassed us. Harassment in every house, set heavy taxes per head, all but the Bhunyas hid in the forest in the end. Knowing that no cronies of Dinu Thakur were hanging around here, they brought elephants from the landowner of Patke and levelled their home. The state repossessed the land. The Thakurs told a python—Mother's familiar, of course—to guard the house. It's still there. Sometimes it leaves the grounds, catches a goat or hen, huge in size. A feud between my father and Dinu Thakur's? Not a thing. Not a thing, just bad talk from bad people. Did Dinu Thakur live in the village, that anyone would have any connections with him? Feud? Oh no. That hanging sentence of Thakur's son, the police brutality, that's why bad suspicion entered Dinu Thakur's father's mind. That his son was caught through Badan Khan from town and my father. If this was true, then my dad would have got as much cash as Badan Khan! All lies. Grown-up son, why didn't you control him? Why should I speak of others? My eldest son Nobne also believes these words.

Sadananda Bhunya's *version* gives us some information about Dindayal Thakur. Not everything.

Nabin Bhunya's *version* is very brief. Yes, Dindayal Thakur's a freedom martyr, I know, I've heard he was hanged trying to loot a train in Kharagpur in 1924. Perhaps it's written in some book somewhere. I don't know. We need a road. Now. Then the village is connected to the outside world. I foam at the mouth talking about this road. I've said that we don't need *labour*. The people of our seven villages will build the road at a quarter of the *labour charge*. The Santhal tribals go often to do piece *labour*. Dasu Soren's bunch know all about *road labour*. They'll give *labour*. The road is needed. Then we can take everything from the village outside, at speed. We also want a *health centre*. Even now a snake-bite is Mother Manosha, cholera is Goddess Badam, and water-magic a fever remedy. The *health centre* is seven miles away. There are more villages behind our village. They also benefit if we get a *health centre* here. Not much, you know, just 70,000 rupees will build a seven mile road, a *health centre*, I'll give the rooms. We can get a *primary school*. With government support we can dredge the tank cut by my forefathers in the thin stream of the Karnabati and make its water usable. Dindayal Thakur? Feud with our family? Of course. There was reason. But I can't say why what happened. No. Don't ask. Snake? In their lot? Hey, you can find cheetahs in winter, and no snakes? Told it to watch their place? Who knows? The ones who say it must've got it from the python. Our palace? Didn't you see? Huge palace, the king repairs spades, the prince thrashes kids. In our village, d'ye hear me, we first need a road. *School.* Studying. The boys can't even get to Patke because there's incredible mud in the rainy season. Ev—erything will follow if there's a road.

One understands from Nabin Bhunya's words that his enthusiasm is not for the past but for the present. He has little enthusiasm for the freedom martyr from the village and he is unwilling to open his mouth about the feud between his family and the Thakur family. His chief concern is how to make the government spend 70,000 rupees, lift dead Chhatim village from archaic and twentieth-century hearsay and half-truths and join modern times by way of a road. *Health centre, school,* road—*buses,* bicycles and open mini-vans will run. Nabin doesn't care for the past.

Nabin cares about one person from the past. This person is a decrepit old woman. The old woman sits in a single-room hut past the courtyard of the Bhunya house. She looks like the Manosha-crone of myth. White hair, torn clothes, emaciated body. Only the eyes have something that tugs at your mind. Her room is quite large. There is a broad dais in it. Nabin comes to this room. For about 10 years now. Before that he too threw stones at the old woman, called her 'witch' and ran off.

Then he found out that the old lady is not a witch. His aunt, his Pishi. His father's sister. In some distant past this aunt *generated* unthinkable events as a result of looking at a bridegroom in her widow's white clothes from under a distant rain tree. So she was marked as misfortune in the Bhunya household. Rather than kill her physically they kept her in a room raised on the yard's far side. For the wives of Pishi's two brothers, Nabin's father's two elder brothers' wives, said that their children would die by the breath of this inauspicious misfortune, this sister-in-law.

Pishi earns her keep. Even at 78 years of age she binds kindling in creepers, drags it and puts it at the other edge of the yard. Nabin's mother or sister gives Pishi some rice–salt–oil–lentil at month's end, two saris yearly. At least that's what Nabin knows. It's Nabin who brings her a bit of hair oil or a loose-weave washcloth from the household provision. He looks out for her in his busy day. The family is fiercely angry at him. Nabin's mother says, behind her son's back, The witch poured ashes on the family and is now making my son a stranger.

These days they're getting an opportunity to show their rage. Because of his constant conflict with his father, Nabin moves about outside the house, and sleeps at the residence of another part-owner of the property. So the amount of rice and lentils decreases and becomes irregular now. Pishi makes no protest. Long ago, a long time back, she forgot to protest against others' behaviour towards herself. She has accepted hunger pangs as *chronic* and unalterable reality. She died, possibly, long ago. From earliest consciousness she remembers that she was at once unwanted and indispensable in the household. Her mother had children yearly, their family was enormous. The Sadananda who carries on the silent torture with his wife and younger son, was, how strange, raised in her arms from birth. Her mother had childbed fever. It seems unreal to think all this now. Does she belong to this house? If close kin, then why outcast? If not kin, then why is she in the house? If the decision is not to feed her, then why give? If one feels like feeding, why give such a small amount of rice? These are most complicated questions. She often weaves a net in her mind with the questions, is herself caught in the net and gives up.

Sometimes she seems very busy. *Necessity* is supposed to be the mother of *invention*. Pushed by that *necessity* she does a lot of work. In a corner of the room the floor is dug up to make a hearth. There she keeps a fire going. Burns wood and makes charcoal. She lights the charcoal and keeps the fire going. Two reasons. First reason is that a box of matches is for her a luxury beyond reach. She never gets money, so the idea of buying matches does not arise. If Nabin thinks of it he gives her matches or hair oil. But he thinks of it only sometimes. Doesn't think of it *regularly* and even then doesn't remember. She has understood, therefore, that it is more intelligent to keep the box of matches in a jar and keep the fire going. The second reason is that with her belly always empty or three-quarters empty, there is nothing left in her body. She likes the fire's warmth and for lack of blood feels chilled all the time. She sits by the fire even in Baishakh and Jaishtha, the high summer months.

Nabin asks, Are you crazy?

Why? What have I done?

Such heat, so hot, and you're sitting by the fire?

Warmth?

The word 'warmth' blossoms and falls like a distressed flower. Her eyes become the sinless stars of dawn and she looks very lovely for an escaping moment. Nabin feels an amazing empathy and attraction. A lot of warmth. Pishi, he says, you feel such cold because you have nothing in your body.

Sometimes she can be seen wandering in the dense impenetrable jungle of the Thakur homestead. She can be seen means the python sees her. Yesterday's orchard is today's jungle. She brings a ripe nona-fruit,[6] an olive, a myrobalan out of this dense overgrowth, driven by the impossible urge to continue living. Nabin knows that Pishi eats whatever she gets. Knowing this, various emotions arise in his breast. *When I start earning I'll screw my dad and take Pishi to* town. *I make no money, but will I never? I still eat my father's food, I won't forever. Pishi has survived so desperately for so long, anyone else would have died. Won't she last a few years longer?*

Sometimes she is seen wandering near the Manosha shrine. She solves her life's problems in various ways. Sometimes people leave milk and water in clay pots as thank offerings at the shrine. She collects the pots. For one reason alone. Once when she was driven out she was given a pot to cook in, a frying bowl. That pot and bowl vanished long ago. She solves her utensil problems by collecting pots this way. The pots are Manosha's, her own clan goddess's. She never thinks of it. Nabin has promised to buy her pots and bowls when he gets a job.

Sometimes you see her, in the hot month of Chaitra, in early evening, far from the village, plucking ripe branches of lentils at speed from someone else's field. For one reason alone, to solve the food problem.

She looks unearthly then. Thin frame, the winds of Chaitra in her white hair, a rapt look in her eyes. That rapt look is seen often and Nabin worries. Pishi has borne injustice all her life, perhaps she is thinking of that, he thinks. In fact she doesn't think of the past. She, too, believes in the present, as does Nabin. She thinks with dream-rapt eyes, when she lies down at night with the lentil seeded and wrapped in her cloth, how slowly she'll eat them in the dark. In fact, all her thoughts are belly-

6 Wild custard apple.

centred. When she dreams, she dreams crude dreams. In
her dream she wears a whole cloth and eats a full serving
of rice in a bell-metal plate. Every day. Only rice. No
lentils, no vegetables. Only rice.

She is the source of Dindayal's martyrdom in 1924,
of the forced departure of the Thakur family, their feud
with the Bhunya family, the arousal of new interest on the
subject of Dindayal in 1978, all. She doesn't recall this.
Just as she doesn't recall that her name was Brajadulali
and once she was as diffident and blooming as a fully
flowering fragrant and white kamini tree.[7]

No one wanted information from her, but she alone
can recount the unwritten account behind Dindayal's
martyrdom.

Once in a great while she leaves behind the clamour
of the Manosha fair and goes to the abandoned river-bed,
on the last day of the rainy month of Sraban, when the
sky casts a kohl-blue shadow, and in the gaps of the white
bonshiuli herb,[8] on the surface of the river-bed, one sees
cheerful clusters of the yellow kadamba.[9] She can't say
why she goes. She sits on a flat stone. Then she doesn't
look human. She doesn't remember the stories she heard
from her father in her childhood. Once a—ll this was
ours. Year round there was deep water in the Karnabati
then. The pollen of the kadam falls on her thin body. She
thinks and thinks. Then she forgets the past glory of the
Bhunya family and thinks, Ripe kadam tastes good. I'll
crush some and take it. I'll put some salt in the tart
kadam and eat it with rice.

7 Night-flowering tree.
8 Fragrant wild flower.
9 Flowery, fruit-bearing tree.

She hasn't known, no one told her at first, that a statue of Dindayal Thakur was about to be established in Chhatim village.

2

The main motive force behind the renewed attention of the administration to the martyred Dindayal Thakur 54 years after his hanging was a bunch of mice and a light-hearted young jail clerk with too much time on his hands, and researchers' interest in preparing a summary of armed revolutionary struggles against the British in the twentieth century. The object was to win a doctorate.

A researcher went to write a doctoral thesis on the neglected events of the history of the armed struggles in Midnapore district. And he poured over jail records at the same time. His cousin, a jail clerk, discovered that mice were gnawing through a lot of 1920–24 records. At his cousin's request he copied whatever he could rescue from those files.

And so he discovered that the martyr Dindayal Thakur was the inhabitant of Chhatim village in Midnapore. He even discovered a long letter written by Dindayal just before his hanging. All the expected stuff such as giving blood to the motherland—quotations from Nazrul's poems[10]—was to be found in the letter. But the most surprising thing was that, halfway to the end, nation, terrorism and lines from the Gita disappear. After a page-and-a-half of this stuff, the remaining six-and-a-half pages are an avowal of love to the 'Dulali' to whom this letter was written. For example—If I'd known,

10 Nazrul Islam (1899–1976), popular Bengali poet whose lyrics are widely sung.

if I could have found the courage, I would have gone away with you. You were too afraid, Dulali. You denied everything. Today I'm on my way to respond to the call of the other shore, if only I could take you along.

Who says life ends at widowhood? Who says there can be no marriage between a Bhunya and a Thakur? Dulali, Dulali, I would have regretted nothing if I could have seen you once, I have not appealed and will not appeal my impending sentence of death by hanging. But at the other end I will wait for you, until we meet again.

Then it is written, You and I wanted nothing more than each other. Even that this heartless society will not allow. I call you, Dulali! Dulali! Can you hear me?

One day, sitting on a stone on the Karnabati river-bed, you had said, Dinu-da, let's take poison. But we hadn't the courage. We didn't do it because both families would have been shamed. Today I ask, Why didn't we? Will they give you this letter? Who knows? Dulali . . . now it seems to me that I always loved you, was it because I didn't know my own heart that I gave or received so much pain?

Two things are obvious from the letter. Loving 'Dulali', Dindayal Thakur had faced some ferocious opposition from rural society, and he loved this woman. It seems as if unrequited love and participation in revolutionary activities were interdependent.

The researcher becomes highly interested. He looks at official reports on the subject of Dindayal.

The defendant is 24, height five foot eleven, skin light, hair coppery and cut short. Brahman, wears the sacred thread. Knows some English, Bengali well. Exceedingly reticent, and it hadn't been possible to make him speak at the police precinct, in the lockup, and at the Central Police Station in Lalbazar, Calcutta.

In December 1924, at seven in the evening, Dindayal Thakur, Ramani Santra and Sardeb Panda stopped the No. 313 'up' train not too far from Kharagpur (the train was carrying postal money) and entered the guard's room saying 'Bande Mataram'. Dindayal said, We're taking money for Mother India's work. Money that a foreign government has taken from us by exploitation, don't stop us.

As a result of this brief announcement (1) the train-robbers could be *categorized* as *terrorists*; (2) some time passes; (3) the armed guards get time to cock their rifles; (4) consequently the armed guards and the train guard are wounded by Dindayal's bullets. And now disaster strikes. Four white officers of a Calcutta merchant company were travelling on this very train. They had guns, for they were going for a shoot in Orissa. They entered the stage armed and helped *arrest* the three revolutionaries. The most significant thing to happen was that all three resisted tooth and nail and, before anyone knew what's what, Dindayal attempted to shoot himself in the temple with his revolver. One of the white men hit his arm and the bullet lodged in his ribs. He was taken wounded to Kharagpur hospital, the other two to Midnapore Jail. Finally, Dindayal had to be taken to Calcutta. First his bullet wound healed there. Then three officers with a reputation for extracting confessions from revolutionaries failed to get a word out of Dindayal. But the other two were younger, information was pressed out of them with the usual physical pokes, needle pricks, trampling with hobnailed boots, etc. Dindayal Thakur was not always a revolutionary. He was recruited in August 1924. Between August and December 3rd he had looted two post offices in the area and snatched the gun of a treasury guard. He's the son of apolitical Chhatim village. There follows a brief trial. There was evidence of the *terrorist* movement in Bengal through Gopinath Shaha's assassination attempt on a white man, mistakenly taking him for Charles Tegart, Commissioner of Calcutta Police. Tegart now forbade spreading news of the Dindayal event too widely. He said one event would *trigger* another. *Try and hang him as an ordinary criminal.* Since there was an order to '*hang*' before 'trying', the Judge had it easy. Dindayal was captured on the 9th and hanged on the 30th. He is highly relieved to hear a death sentence and is hanged in the usual fearless way of the terrorists. *Funeral by police.* After Dindayal is hanged, the police come to Chhatim village in mid-January.

The researcher is delighted. The state is looking for freedom fighters everywhere; here's a freedom fighter. He creates interest in the administration. Consequently an old guy in his 70s receives an allowance from that state as Dindayal's only living relative. The researcher publishes his book, and he, too, is given a D.Phil. among others at the *convocation* of the University in the style in which fried *puris*[11] are thrown carelessly at rows of wedding guests waiting to be fed. Since his book doesn't sell, he himself distributes it everywhere. He had published it at his own expense, so there's no problem. The book reaches a certain Minister's office and the Minister's Personal Assistant is *electrified* upon perusing it. A freedom fighter, a *genuine* martyr, a martyr from Midnapore, the proper cradle of revolution, yet nothing has been done with him! He is able to explain the need for erecting a statue of Dindayal to his Minister. Since the statue of a dead man

---

11 Ball of flour rolled into a circular shape and made to swell up by being deep fried.

is much more important than other living problems, there is no difference of opinion about the decision to erect a statue.

Sadan Khan enters at this *stage*. His grandfather was a passenger on the No. 313 'up' on the 9th in 1924. Badan Khan had identified Dindayal at the time of capture and, travelling to Calcutta, had helped the police at a *later stage*. His star was on a climb since then and it is for this reason that his son Madan Khan was marked as a patriot after Independence. Now Sadan Khan comes forth in some way and shows interest in the matter of the statue.

There is slight friction about the material of the statue. Not stone. Even the lion cub of Birsingha village[12] was not able to keep its head intact because the statue was of stone.

If not stone, clay?

If you don't cover it, a clay statue will melt in water, if you do it'll be a nest of termites, Sadan says.

Bronze?

At this stage someone jokes, Bronze is good. There's money in it if you break it and sell it in bits.

This pains Sadan Khan greatly. Hey? What did you say? Such a good son of our country, who will break his statue and sell? We may be from a country town but we're not inhuman!

Thus the decision is to build it in bronze. Sadan's efforts unearth a 1918 *school magazine* of Surajmohini

12 Birsingha was the birthplace of the great intellectual and reformer Iswarchandra Vidyasagar (1820–91). Satyendranath Dutta, the Bengali nationalist poet, called him 'the lion cub of Birsingha'.

Boys' School. There you get a *photo* of Dindayal Thakur who got a *First Division* from the school in the college entrance exams. The sculptor is shown the *photo* and told, This is an eighteen-year old, raise the age of the statue by six years. Hearing this the sculptor is blown away. But he says nothing, if he loses the *contract*, the loss is his. He says, *Yes sir* and leaves.

Sadan Khan returns to town and gives Nabin the good news. Says, I heard they've printed a letter written to Aunt Duli in the book. The reporters might ask.

What will they ask?

Think about it. With parents alive, why did Dinu Thakur write to your Pishi?

When Nabin came back to the village and imparted this piece of news his dad was exceedingly enraged and Nabin too got heated.

Why get angry?

No, I'll dance for joy.

Why're you angry?

All you do at home is eat. Home gossip gets out and I won't be mad?

Baba, times have changed.

Nothing has changed in the villages.

No, there won't be any trouble.

No problem?

When Sadananda went to town Sadan Khan also said, What an idea! Reporters will ask questions. You tell them we don't know to whom he wrote a letter. Keep Aunt Duli away. Don't let her appear in front of anyone. Then all will be quiet.

Treason begins at home: my dear Nabin?

I'll explain to him.

Nabin was truly angry now. He said, I'll cover up nothing. Then it was a scandal, now no one will think of that. You can't just give orders from *town*. I will keep pace with them. Without a paved road, seven villages remain in darkness. Will that work get done if we put our shoulders together to the task? You get things done these days if you write in the newspaper.

The topic of all this discussion was looking for ripe myrobalan in the dead bed of the Karnabati. She was pulling her creeper-tied bundle of twigs from site to site. Nabin found her right there as he cycled searching.

Pishi! he cried out.

Who's that? Nabin?

What're you doing in this dense jungle?

Hey, it's ripe myrobalans, have one?

Pishi came up pulling her bundle of twigs behind her.

Nabin says, Sit down here.

Why?

I must talk.

With me?

Who else do I talk to at home? Are they human?

Why? Does your dad scold you?

Forget them. Sit.

Nabin takes Pishi's hand and sits her down. I'm trying so hard, he says, won't I get a job, Pishi? Whatever I get I'll blow my horn in your brother's face and take you away.

Always the same thing, Nabin!

What'd you think I've brought for you?

Hair oil?

I forgot. Sorry.

That's all right.

Nabin wrapped a cloth around her. Bought for seven rupees at the *town* market. A thin piece of cloth, hardly any thread count. But Pishi is dressed in rags, and Nabin's purse doesn't run to much. Pishi was in bliss.

Oh Nabin, for me? What a lovely colour, how warm, smell its new smell?

I know. Take this.

What's in the box?

Gout ointment. There were hawkers on the bus. You groan all the time with knee pain and lower back pain?

Where'd you get the money? Your dad?

Of course not! I don't go to *town* for nothing. Murari-babu from Patke has a printing press. I'm learning that work a bit.

Because your dad gives you nothing?

No. What's there to give?

Yet all the land is temple land. Your share is as much as Sada's, as your brother's.

No, Pishi, I don't want anything from them. Nabin sat for a while with Pishi's hand in his hand. Three o'clock on a winter afternoon. Sand blows over the dry river-bed. You can hear the distant water-buffalo bells ringing. Dasu Soren's group is sowing the spring harvest on the river-bed. All around are the wave upon wave of the *laterite zone*; the murmur of the fall of leaves in the dwarf-Sal forests. Desolate, melancholy-making afternoon. Nabin wants to bind this silent indifference in a paved road and take it into the lap of the present.

Pishi's white hair, soft and sad loneliness in her thin face, lined skin. In Dindayal's letter you read of her standing with her lean hip cocked, of her astonishing beauty—Nabin has read it in town. Now what he has to say to Pishi is most cruel. But the era that Nabin wants to bring to Chhatim village is heartless and unforgiving. The reporters won't leave Pishi alone.

Pishi, one word—

Tell me.

Do you remember Dinu Thakur?

Pishi is speechless. She places her helpless eyes on Nabin's and he notices amazed for the first time that, although Pishi is 78, her eyes are still alive.

Do you remember, Pishi?

Yes.

Dinu Thakur's name is in a book, Pishi.

Where?

I don't have it.

Then?

Your name, too.

My name!

Dinu Thakur wrote you a letter before being hanged. That letter is printed in a book.

What'll happen, Nabin?

What'll happen to what?

Where'll I go if your dad sends me away?

No one's going to send you away. Listen.

Tell me.

There'll be a statue of Dinu Thakur in the village.

Where?

Their place will be cleared. There.

When?

I hear in three months. Then people will come, they might ask you some things.

What shall I say?

Whatever comes to mind.

Your dad . . .

I, too, have rights, Pishi, you said yourself. Who's going to blame you? If they do, you and I will go to town, we'll starve and see if we live or die.

Nabin . . .

What?

Your uncle, younger than me, now he's dead, he beat me a lot then. All the trouble, all my suffering, started then . . . but everyone had forgotten that stuff, again . . .

Pishi! Don't think of what happened then.

How many years ago?

Fifty-four.

Fifty-four? So long ago?

Yes, Pishi.

Your dad knew nothing. He was a tiny boy then. He too is grown up now . . . your ma . . . I'm thrown in a corner with less power than field-cattle.

I know.

Today, after such a long time . . .

Don't think of it. No one will say a thing. I'm on the Panchayat.[13] There must be some respect for my word in the village? No one will object. Come, let's go home.

---

13 Village-level self-governing unit.

Let's go.

Hey, I keep forgetting. Here.

What, dear?

Five hundred grams ground chickpea and treacle.

Long life my love, bless you my love. A king's ransom for you.

Kings and queens! They don't even give you a handful of rice. And you wish a king's ransom for me?

All right, don't be king.

Pishi, the police evicted the entire Thakur family?

They did. And . . .

Yes?

Big brother, angry with me . . .

Let it go. Don't cry.

Tell your dad, Nabin, not to torture me any more. I'm ready to live in a shack upon this river-bed in the woods.

Always the same. Stop it.

3

She had thought to have remembered nothing. But at night, pulling the straw door to and lying down on the platform, she remembered everything. How? She was not supposed to remember. All the disasters in her life are from that event. Is that why she hasn't forgotten? So many days, so many years, everything was buried somewhere. Nabin came as the North wind and blew away all the leaves today.

How long, how long ago?

Both were born with the century. Of the same age, of the twentieth century. But the twentieth century did not accept them as friends. It left them in the Middle Ages and went on ahead.

Suddenly she realized that she could not reach the mind, the love, of those days, of the two she was thinking of, any more. At 78, the body becomes such that today's unappeased hunger appears much more real than the unrequited love of the past. It's impossible to become the Brajadulali of that time (in the mind) and to go back into the past. Possible rather to look back at the Brajadulali and Dindayal of that time as another girl, another boy, from a distance.

She thought of this because of Nabin. Nabin speaks to her, she sees the present through Nabin's eyes. Another reason is the peculiarity of her mode of existence in this family. She always wanders in wood and wilderness. She sees, and once in a long while speaks to, Dasu Soren's group, and the Bauri caste, and Ratan the barber. She knows they will not report these conversations to Nabin's father and brother. For many reasons they think of the Bhunyas as enemy, and of Nabin as friend. She herself also thinks that they want what Nabin wants. Paved road, health centre, market-place—that's good. She finds no connection between their good and any good-happenings for herself. In fact, she thinks of herself as dead. At this age, undone by ceaseless worry about food, she cannot think of anything more good than today's chickpea powder, tomorrow's crushed parched rice. Dasu Soren often gives her a custard apple, a jujube or two and says, Your problem is that you're a king's daughter. Nothing to eat, yet you can't beg, most dangerous. Dasu Soren often says that belonging to a royal family has been her bane.

At that time Dasu's father Kanu Soren sharecropped the Bhunya's land. The Thakur's land as well. Thinking of

Brajadulali he could in no way remember her wedding. Vain effort. At four the wedding in the Bhunya house in Patke, at six a widow. As far as memory goes, Brajadulali is wearing widow's white. Brajadulali never wore shellac bangles, saris with borders, silver fish-pins in her hair, anklets on her legs—the Bhunyas behaved like the priestly brahman Thakurs. They were respected in the village for this.

Dulali never addressed Dinu with a show of respect. There was no cause to. From the age of 10 Dulali would go to Dinu's mother. A widowed daughter, a lovely daughter, Dulali's mother made her do many rituals all year. At the end of these, instead of saying:

May I be wife forever

With a bright-shiny home of husband and son

May I die with my hair-part vermilion

Dulali would say:

Father's house full to bursting

Brother's house bright and shining

As long may they live

As the hairs on my head.

The two met all the time. Every day. Dulali was the landowner's daughter. Although the king was now just a farming householder, the village people still gave respect. A village daughter, Dulali wandered everywhere at ease. Because Dinu's mother was always busy, because Dinu's two sisters were tiny heaps, it was Dulali who mended the clothes of Dinu's father, Dinu himself and Dinu's brothers. It was she who put covers on Dinu's books. No one knew how to make ink from ink tablets then. Dinu's father would say, No one knows how to make ink from inkstone like Dulali. Both of them said, Such grace in her limbs. Why was such a beautiful, wonderful girl born in that house, and why such evil fate, who knows?

Uncle used to talk, and Dulali would hear vaguely. Uncle would say that if Dulali had been married two months later, she would not have been widowed. Dulali, oh dear how shameful. At 12 she went to the wedding of a special friend. Kusum's aunt turned her out with, Out, out! Fearing the Bhunyas, Kusum's mother said to her, Duli! You're not to see a wedding, dear, you're not to join in the wife-rites. Come and see when Kusi goes to her groom's house in the palki.[14]

Dulali came home and said to her mother with angry tears, Why did you have my wedding, then? I wouldn't be a widow if you'd done it later. I couldn't see Kusi's wedding.

Four years later, it was another wedding day, the day Kusi's younger sister Malati was getting married. Everyone went from her house, Dulali stood alone behind the house, standing on her toes, holding the Champak tree branch, listening to the wedding music. She hadn't realized that Dinu had come up and was standing beside her. She was startled when he spoke, with a sudden start of fear.

What are you listening to?

Ohh! It's you!

What're you listening to?

Wedding music. Did you go?

No.

Why? Don't you want to see the groom? They've sat the groom in the other uncle's house, haven't they?

14 Simple village palanquin.

I don't know.

What do you need?

I've been looking at you.

At me? Why, all of a sudden?

Why sudden? I look at you all the time.

That you do, yes, but . . .

What happened next was most unexpected. Dinu put his finger on her face, drew it down and said, You look like Saraswati, the Goddess of Learning.

What is this?

Look, I love you, so I want to touch you a bit.

Dulali is very afraid. Her face gets hot, her body trembles. Then she says, You go to school in Patke, is this what you're learning?

Do they teach this in school?

Go, go away now.

Dulali herself ran away. She went into her room and shut the door. She lay on her front, put her face in her pillow, trembled and trembled, and then fell quiet. Then she got up, and very carefully looked at her face in the glass. Clear light skin, a lovely face, this she has known forever. Mother says, Don't look in the mirror, dear. So Dulali doesn't look in the mirror, doesn't braid her hair, just winds it on her fingers and puts it up anyhow. She doesn't do the widow's fast on the eleventh day of the moon's phase, just eats chickpea powder with milk and banana. At night she eats puffed rice, milk and bananas.

I love you! What a terrible sentence, how full of unease. From childhood Dulali has learnt to fear the word 'love'.

Charan Bauri's wife from the Bauri quarter had love with her husband's younger cousin. There was bloodshed in the Bauri quarter. The Panchayat had said that there couldn't be violence in the village because of this. A god-fearing village. Brahmans live there. Charan must get rid of his cousin. Why has he kept him, seeing as he is a homeless orphan?

Charan's wife came to their house to get paddy. Quite disoriented, disaster was written all over her face. Everyone in the house looked at her with great curiosity, Dulali as well. Charan's wife looked at everyone with a piercing glance. Then she took her paddy and left. She went home, boiled the paddy, carefully tended the earth floor of the yard, then went off to bathe in the river-bed. The rainy month of Sraban, there was water in the river-bed. She did not return home. She and her husband's cousin ate the poisonous seed of the trumpet flower and died together. In the depth of the woods. There was a lot of talk about this in village life. Fear entered Dulali's heart. What is love like? Love means violence in the community, death?

There is fear in the word 'love'. Dulali's first cousin loved his wife, so his mother treated her daughter-in-law with incredible cruelty. Dulali's father used to say, What's the use of so much love and friendship? You've come to work in this world, do it. Marrying, having children is also the world's work. There is no good in loving. This daughter-in-law lost her mind later. Her aunt sent her back to her father and arranged another marriage for Dulali's cousin.

Dinu loves her? How? Does anyone love someone whom he's seen all his life? Love starts when a new bride returns to her husband from her first ritual visit home after the wedding. When you see someone for the first time. Dulali decides she hasn't caught Dinu's meaning. He loves her as he has seen her forever, like a sister. She's a widow so she can't see a wedding, pained by her pain he had come to her.

It was the month of Sraban. Dulali puts some milk at the shrine every day. That day, too, she had put the milk down, touched her head to the ground, and was returning fast. It started raining on the way, she was wet through. She ran and stood under a tree. Then she saw Dinu coming home with an umbrella over his head.

O Dinu! Stop a bit.

Dulali? You?

I was at the shrine.

Come, come under my umbrella.

Stop a bit, it's raining too hard.

Let's stop, then.

The two of them under an umbrella. The sky dark with clouds. Who'll say it's afternoon, looks like night. Dulali was most uncomfortable.

Dinu said suddenly, Dulali!

What?

What have you done to me, Dulali! I can't think of anything but you.

Don't say it, be quiet.

Why did you come to be Mahananda Bhunya's daughter? Why were you widowed?

Dulali, distraught with terror, said, Aren't you Priest-uncle's son? Aren't you brahman? You are not to say such things to me!

Dulali ran off that day. But now she can't even explain anything to herself. She says, enraged, to her mother, You know I'm going to the shrine. Milk in one hand, bananas in the other. Couldn't you have sent someone with me with an umbrella?

She is in a bad fix. She goes to the Thakur house a number of times every day. With fruit, with milk, to get dishes cooked by Thakur-aunt. How can she say, I won't go? People will suspect something. Gossip will grow with word of mouth. Thinking of all this she forgets to dry her hair. She has fever in the morning.

She had very high fever. What people call pneumonia fever. It was Dinu who brought a doctor from Patke. Mother put poultices on her chest and wept. Father would say, Get well my darling. You light up our house. My Dulali, I can forget everything when I see your face.

She got well but she didn't get her strength back for a long time. At last, on the last day of Bhadra, the next month, she took her brother Sadananda on her hip and went to pick thankuni herb by the pond. Dinu came by. He said nothing, she neither. Dulali's heart was pounding. She picked her thankuni somehow and came away. Dinu appeared in the evening. He sat in a cane chair in the yard and said, Aunt, look at your girl's conduct. Here she was sick, I brought a doctor from Patke. She got well, she didn't say a word? Mother sent this water. She gave God some tulsi[15] water in her name.

Dulali came out at her mother's shout. She touched his feet at her mother's behest. Dinu said, Now come, my lady. Mother's waiting on your Highness' pleasure with some food from our home shrine.

15 Mint, considered an auspicious plant.

Go Dulali. Shameful, she's waiting! Go quickly.

Dulali had to go. Dinu said, So? See I made you well?

You made me well?

Didn't I call the Lord every day?

Dinu.

What?

Don't talk like that.

Why?

I hurt.

I hurt, too.

What can I do about that? Please be calm. I am of low caste, and then a widow. You are getting education; the eldest son of the house, you will be married.

We'll see.

You are uncle's strength and hope.

We'll see.

Tell me you'll calm down.

Will you be pleased if I calm down?

I'll be at peace.

You'll be at peace, Dulali? At peace? Good. Then I'll calm w—ay down. I won't bother you any more. Dulali, stand here, let me look at you. Duli, Dulali, Dulali, I love you so much, I never got the chance to say it.

Running, almost running, Dinu went away. From there, from the village. Told his father, I won't be a priest like you. I'll go to school. It's hard for me to travel back and forth from the village. I'll live in Patke at my brother-in-law's house.

Dinu didn't come to the village for a long, long time. He left, giving Dulali peace and a great deal of pain. He returns after eight months. On the day of the Manosha fair. Hundreds of people in Chhatim village that day, the village is agog since dawn with people, water-buffalo-carts, and pouring rain. Dulali went to the fair. Dinu called her to the Karnabati river-bed. What's happening to me, Dulali? he said. I can't forget you, no way, what's this?

I, too, haven't forgotten.

Dulali had spoken. In 1917 Dinu and Dulali, both 17, were no longer minors. They knew the responsibility of all adult emotions. Knowing the consequences, Dulali had said, I, too, haven't forgotten.

The time was ineffable. A time to say the whole truth. Twilit dusk, the sky dark, in the background the roaring music of the Manosha shrine. There will be a recital of the Tale of Manosha at night. In front the roar of the groundwater pouring down the incline of the sand-bank of the dead river-bed. The fragrance of kadam on the wind. The world was slow with cloud, the wind was lightning-struck in some unknown anticipation.

You haven't forgotten? Then come close.

Dulali had gone to him. Then she had raised her face and said, First listen to me, Dinu.

With a most stern face, and slowly, Dulali had said, I love you but what's the good?

What's to lose?

What's the use Dinu? You will not be able to say this to people. I won't either.

No.

All you'll get is pain.

Yes.

Then what's the good?

I don't know.

Dinu.

Hmm?

We could both die.

Hush.

Then tell me you'll forget me?

But I can't forget.

What can I say, then?

There's nothing to say, nothing.

They stood quiet for a long time. Then Dinu said, Let's see. This Chhatim is not the universe. You go back. We won't go together. People will talk.

Dinu goes to Patke again. He sits for his school-leaving exams next year. He goes to Kharagpur before the *results* are out. Dinu's father knew that Dinu was in Kharagpur. But Dinu went to Calcutta with the Bengali teacher of Patke School. This teacher must have had a great effect on Dinu. For the Dinu who came back to the village after the exam results were out was a different Dinu. Spare of speech, stern and serious. At this time he went around in the fisherfolks' neighbourhoods, the Bauri quarter, in the cholera season. He worked in rural relief. When cholera was contained, the *Health Inspector* came from Kharagpur, praised Dinu and said at the local police station before he returned, Start with village relief, end with *terrorism*, I've seen a lot. The Police Inspector gave no importance to this and said, Poison-root breeds poison trees, can the son of a god-fearing brahman priest turn out bad?

Dinu makes no attempt to see Dulali. As if he'll get no peace if he doesn't spend himself completely, he now starts work with malaria prevention. Dulali also shrinks into herself. This is good, this is very good. She doesn't go to learn any rituals anymore. She keeps herself immersed in household chores. But when everyone is at the temple for the worship of the harvest Kali, he calls her into the garden of their house. He says, Dulali, I now know everything.

What?

I'll marry you.

Marry? Me?

I'll marry you.

Aren't you afraid of sinning?

What sin? Widows can remarry, by law. What fear? We'll go to Calcutta. A hundred thousand people and more, a huge city, who will find us? I'm telling you, Dulali, marry me, hold me, otherwise I'll float away.

Then let me die, Dinu.

Die—die—can't you say 'I'll live'?

How'll I say that? If I go with you it'll be scandal, the blacklist, my father will be fallen.

He'll do a penance and reclaim caste.

I'll not forget, I'll burn out.

You won't be able to?

No.

Do you love me?

Yes.

Still . . .

I don't have that courage.

What can I tell you then?

There is nothing to say. Our castes don't match, I'm a widow, everyone in the village . . . respected line . . . shame . . .

Then go.

Go?

Go. Never come in front of me, never.

Dulali wanted to die that day. Dulali didn't know what strong attraction pulled him, Dinu couldn't hold himself firm.

Dinu became a schoolteacher in Patke. I will not sit in the village and be the Bhunya's priest, Father. Tell him whatever you like.

It was a great blow to Thakur-uncle. Is it right to say, 'I won't do' my clan-work, caste-duty?

Get married and go.

I won't marry.

In 1919, no 19-year-old village boy could say this to his father's face. Mother had said, You hurt your dad?

He has another son.

Why have you changed so?

I won't tell you.

Dinu left. But fate did not allow them to be still. A fate self-created by them. Dinu fell ill in Patke, high delirium. He couldn't be brought back to the village. His mother went there to nurse him. Came back a few days later in a water-buffalo-cart. She said to Dulali's mother, eyes swollen with tears, Kadu! What I say is for my son's sake. My Dinu won't last long. He calls Duli all, all the time. Sister, don't think of your modesty or mine, he calls in delirium. He calls you, he calls my Bhunya brother-in-law, there seems to be something he wants to say.

Dulali's father says, Let's go, sister-in-law. And to Dulali's mother, You come too. If you don't and Dinu doesn't last, we will be touched by a brahman's curse. If he doesn't go, then there will be words, why didn't they go to see him?

They are more distressed at the possibility of Dinu's death. Dulali's mother is a simple soul. She says, You won't call Duli? The same midwife delivered them, is this a loose tie?

Dulali enters with her parents and Dinu's mother. Dinu looks with bloodshot eyes and says, Sit there. Get up when I die. A room full of relatives and in-laws. The curiosity in their glance undresses Dulali. Dulali, distraught with shame, fear and pain, sits there like a stone.

Dinu's fever goes in two days. Dulali returned with her family. Dinu's family returns a month later. Then one day Dinu's father calls Dulali's father to his place. A full grown girl, he says, and then a widow, you have to be very careful, Mahananda.

Why?

Dinu's father's eyes are not normal. Somehow the centre of his life has been destabilized. He says, Dinu says widow-remarriage is possible both by scripture and civil law. He will marry Dulali.

Both of them turn to stone by the massive blow of these words.

Then Dulali's father says, You arrange a marriage for your boy, Sir. I will discipline my girl. But what have you just said, Thakur-brother? Is this to be credited? Did the fever addle Dinu's brain?

Don't tell your daughter. What does she know. Maybe the fault is all Dinu's. The word will spread if you tell her.

What will you do to your son?

The question contained the sorrow of a father's broken heart, but also a challenge. My daughter is not guilty, can't be. My darling never wore a bit of colour since childhood, she's never even raised her voice.

It's Dinu's fault doubtless. But Mahananda, a man's guilt can be washed off, not a woman's.

Arrange a marriage for your boy, Sir.

Mahananda returns home afflicted by question and doubt. He tells all to his wife. Then father calls Dulali and says, Don't go to the garden from the house, Dulali, I'm warning you.

I don't go, Baba.

Then why did Thakur-brother say such things? Why did he say Dinu . . . with you . . . ?

I don't know, Baba.

Dulali was getting courage somewhere in her inmost heart. Somewhere she knew she was not guilty. Loving Dinu was not a crime. Explaining this to father and mother was also impossible.

You haven't done anything wrong, have you, little mother?

No, Baba. Nothing wrong.

I knew, I knew.

Then I won't go to the shrine?

Emboldened by his filial love Mahananda is extraordinarily bold. You will. You'll go as you went. My mind tells me you'll do nothing wrong.

Tell Thakur-uncle to take his son from the village, to arrange a marriage. I don't want to hear anything on his account. I'll kill myself if anyone says anything to you.

She is very angry with Dinu for endangering her existence with incredibly immodest proposals even when she has not sinned by loving, when she has accepted the fact that her love will remain unfulfilled. At the same time there is an unbearable pain in her chest. Of joy. Dinu has said in public he'll marry her.

Dinu stood in front of her on her way back from the shrine. Let me go, Dinu.

What did you tell Uncle?

To get you married.

Whom shall I marry, loving you?

Dinu! If you don't marry I'll kill myself. A marriage between you and me is not to be, Dinu. As long as I live, I'll have to depend on my father or my brother, in this village. Do you want to grab my shelter?

Say once you love me.

I love you. You know that too.

Say it again.

With her head held high, Dulali said, regally at ease, I love you, will love you as long as I live. But nothing will come of this love of ours in this life. Get married. Loving you, Dinu . . . I can lie in the dust for you, Dinu. . . if you walk on me my limbs don't hurt . . . if loving you, Dinu, I can ask you to get married, then loving me, can you not have your marriage arranged?

Let me see if I can, Dulali. Let me see.

Let me go.

Go, watch where you go. It's dark.

Dulali comes home. Then one day it was heard that Dinu was going to be married. In that Patke village. With his sister's sister-in-law. His sister's father-in-law had just died. It was heard that Dinu was going to Calcutta. There he would be apprenticed at a printing press. His brother-in-law had fixed it.

Dulali couldn't bear it that day. By the river-bed she climbed on a hillock and clung to a tree. The bullock-cart passed by, Dinu's eye was turned to the village. Dinu didn't see her. She saw him full, filling her two eyes. Face thin with recent illness, light skin, close-cropped hair, a strange smile limned on his lips. A heart-rending smile.

It wasn't easy to fix the wedding day. Finally the wedding was fixed for November of 1924. There was music. A new thatched hut was raised to keep the marriage supplies. It was discovered that the moment for the groom's departure was in the morning. Before midday the groom will start from the house. He will sit beneath an awning under a tree. The groom will start at three in the afternoon.

In winter the sun goes quickly. Mahananda will give all the fish for the wedding feast, all the yoghurt, all the sweets, Mughal gold coins for the bride's trousseau.

Dinu lit up the tree under which he sat. Dulali didn't go, she didn't go all day. She didn't leave her room. She couldn't talk to anyone, yet her heart was breaking. Finally, winding her dry unwashed hair in her hand, pulling the end of her white borderless cloth around her body, Dulali came out step by step. Far away but still you can see him. White silk dhoti, ecru silk shirt, a big shawl around his shoulders, the sandalwood mark of worship on his forehead, flat gold circlets on his ears, this last a lineage custom. Dinu lifts his eyes from there, and sees her. He sees, he gazes, and then he stands up. Then he tears off the wreath from around his neck, throws his shawl down, wipes the mark off his forehead.

Dinu shouts in a terrible voice towards those from the bride's party who'd come to get the groom, Go back home, please. I won't marry. These terrible and terrific words burst and rent the village sky, inaugurated an apocalypse.

Lying on this bamboo platform she can remember everything even after these 54 years. The pictures were arranged in her mind. In her adolescence painters would come to show pictures, unroll the picture slowly, show it, and then sing the narrative of the theme of the picture. Who were those painters, where have they gone, they are lost somewhere like her adolescence and youth.

What painter is sitting in her mind today and showing picture after picture, explaining everything? What a pain in her chest. What weight does memory have, why does it hurt? A great destruction had come down on the village. Even now the pictures are trembling, moving, breaking.

Thakur-uncle had said, You're not my son. Leave right now.

I will, I'll do just that.

Dinu leapt into this house. Screamed and said, Come, Dulali. If we remain in the village after this they will cut you up alive.

Dulali loses consciousness.

Dinu leaves the village. In rage, insult and shame Thakur-uncle throws his wooden sandal at him. His forehead breaks open. The scar helped Badan Khan identify him later.

The village is filled with an unnatural calm. They are all the Bhunyas' tenant farmers. They say nothing. The kings are embattled. Thakur-uncle places a curse on Mahananda. The two families blame each other. Dulali lies forgotten in a corner. There is a search on for Dinu.

Then comes that morning of horror. The noise of Aunt's lamentation from the Thakur house. Dinu has robbed a train, he's been caught, he'll be hanged. O my Dinu-uu-uu!

Then the news of the hanging. Thakur-uncle standing in the courtyard and saying, I return the sacred pitcher, I return the idol. You fed my son to that daughter of yours. I won't perform worship for the god of your house, I won't live on your land. I curse you, may your line die, die, die.

Then police in the village. Elephants came from Patke, and a multitude of policemen. They kicked Thakur-uncle, Aunt and the children out of the house. The rider goaded the elephant, and the elephant demolished the house. Thakur-uncle tells Father, Do nothing. Let everything go. Then he kneels in front of the Police Inspector and says, My son is gone, my house is gone, now please ask your elephant to walk over me, I beg you.

The Inspector screams, What're you doing, please stop, I am only a kayastha by caste.

What am I? Thakur-uncle lifts up his arms as if to address the created universe, What am I?

You're a brahman.

I'm a brahman? Is that why an untouchable hanged my son, and an untouchable burnt him? Your constables drag my wife by the hand? I'm still a brahman? Everyone is uncomfortable at his clamorous grieving, the Inspector too, he goes home without further discussion.

Father clasped Thakur-uncle's feet. Thakur-uncle had said, Your daughter is alive, Mahananda. You have not felt filial bereavement. And still you're thinking of what disaster may come to you. Why should I take your household god? The image? I wish you misfortune, yes. If this brings you tremendous misfortune, perhaps I'll get a bit of peace. You brought me such immense misfortune through your daughter?

Thakur-uncle and his family left, are leaving, the Bauri untouchables and the fishers are moving them, the Bauris and fishers had come to love them. It's said that they spent the nights under trees, the fishers kept watch around them. They moved 42 miles in four days and reached Kharagpur. Some people from the railway colony came under cover and gave them money, bought them tickets. They went to Puri, the seat of the god Jagannath. Then who went where? How do human beings get lost, like Dulali's cursed youth?

At the Bhunya house Mahananda had said, I'll axe Dulali. He, too, is adrift. Loving his daughter, Dinu was banished, seditious, killed on the gallows. Dinu's father is a guileless man, his house has been levelled. The Manosha whose worship is his family duty has been deserted by her priest. The village is under divine rage, royal rage, brahman rage. All due to Dulali. Dulali's mother put a machete in her husband's hands and said, You can't just cut her down, cut me down too. Then, you are a man, have another family.

Everything will be as you say? There's no community?

Has the community asked for her death?

Asked that she be discarded.

Throw her away. I'll go, too. Mother and daughter will live as beggars.

Everything was destroyed because of her, and you still won't let her go?

Who is the community in Chhatim? You are the community. Whatever you say happens. You're giving me community?!

An easy solution was to kill Dulali. But Dulali's mother stops them from inside. An obstacle comes unexpectedly from outside. Dasu Majhi's father Bulan Soren says, Dinu Thakur told us when he left, She's your sister, watch over her. You can't kill her. Then we'll burn everything. We'll find Dinu Thakur's pals and tell them everything.

Mahananda is a householder. He became brutal at a time of a terrible disaster, and came to his senses when obstructed. But he was the head of village society. It is his job to outwit the sins of the home. It is by way of his daughter that the village fell into divine ire.

Dulali is made an outsider at home. This room is raised. She is not allowed to enter the household. There is an arrangement for her upkeep—rice, lentils, oil, salt, wood, paraffin, sari, washcloth. Then the shrine room is raised again after penance. This life since then. As long as Mother was alive, she'd come and sit outside. Mother would weep. Dulali didn't have the strength to weep. Day and night she thought, why didn't I listen to him, why didn't I leave, he had said there is a huge world outside Chhatim. She'd think why, for whose pride and respect, did I say 'no' to him? Dinu was gone, would never come again, for a long time it was piercingly painful to accept this. Then day by day that feeling of pain lessened. Sadananda was then eight.

Today Sadananda is an old man of 62. The head of the house. Where is anyone, where was the Thakur house, where and when did someone, seeing her from a distance, get up saying 'I won't marry', what distant tales. Everything became a lie. The aching belly remained, and the tedium of passing each day.

Her sorrow will end when Nabin gets a job.

She fell asleep. Before she slept she tried to bring to mind the sharp burning passion of that past Dindayal, that past Dulali. No, it's not there. The light is dim in the winter sky, a slight cloud cover, breeze, the smell of ripe aman paddy[16] on the wind, the horn playing, a huge fig tree outside the Thakur house. Under it a shoddy awning. The groom is sitting on a high bench. Fiery complexion, aquiline nose, reddish-black hair, the tilak[17] mark burning on his forehead, ornaments in his ears, a chaplet of marigolds around his neck. A girl is gazing and gazing at him, leaning against a rain tree. She is wearing the plain white cotton sari of a widow. Its end is wrapped around her because it's winter. Her dry hair is roughly wound in a bun. The young woman's eyebrows are arched and long, her nose is slightly short, full lips, her skin the colour of the linseed flower, eyes black, wide open, unblinking. The groom lifts his eyes speaking to someone, his words stop, his mouth opens, it shuts, the groom stands up. He tears the wreath from his neck, throws the shawl from his shoulders. Says, Go back home, please. I won't marry.

Yes, it's a picture of some other Dulali, some other Dinu. The picture is recalled, the picture speaks, but it is no longer possible to be of one mind with them. Fifty-four years is too long a time. Living has happened for too many days, too many. Seventy-eight is too old to be. No

16 Winter paddy.
17 Auspicious mark made on forehead, usually with sandalpaste.

one lives this long. Mother used to say, The body wasn't used, no child was made in your belly, I'll die, Duli, but I am afraid to think how long you'll live.

No one is left in the village from those days. Where are the companions with whom she played hopscotch in childhood, singing

One foot in water

Under the kadam tree

Two feet in water

In hellhole you'll be—?

They are long dead and gone. Where Dinu stood and watched Dulali is now a thick undergrowth of cactus. She has lived too long, time has gone on, leaving her behind. Dinu will remain the same in memory, a handsome young man of 24. And Dulali is now an old woman of 78. And so she walks around. She never kept company with a man in her life. So her body was not quite ruined. Sadananda's daughter broke caste, married a kayastha, meeting him at her maternal uncle's house. Some cousin of Sadananda's has supposedly married an untouchable Kaot woman and settled in Durgapur. The woman is a *nurse*. No one has lost caste this way; there is no shame. What a waste, what useless living. Only Nabin, as forthcoming as Dinu, in the evening of her life, says to his pishi with the same self-confidence that he'll take her into a new life. Evening. Time to pick the flowers of the little gourd, time to listen to fairy tales. The little gourd blossoms in the evening. In Dulali's youth, when hundreds of gourd flowers bloomed on the lattice in the courtyard, Mother would say, Tear off a few, my love. All those flowers will pull at the tree's life, it won't bear fruit.

After picking off the flowers of the little gourd Dulali would sit to prepare oil-lamp wicks. Andimani, an old maidservant, would then gently pat Dulali's younger brothers and sisters to sleep and tell fairy tales. Moonlight was silvery everywhere then. The moon shone on the king's daughter's face. And said right then, I want this daughter!

In the evening of life, at the time of picking the flowers of the little gourd, at the time of listening to fairy tales, Nabin says he'll take her to a new life. Constructing a paved road he will drag a new time into the village by the ear. Make the government build a health centre.

Let them get good fortune, let them. What is Chhatim village guilty of, that it will remain in darkness for so long? Light here is paraffin, music the tin horn and bamboo-stick drum, the road is of dirt, the village quack for snake-bite, Ratan barber's magic for sickness, otherwise a doctor from Patke.

Let them see better days.

4

A few days later Nabin called her. Tell me what you see, he said.

Let's look first.

From the fisherfolks' quarter and Bauri quarter, every villager is clearing the growth from the Thakur house wilderness.

What'll happen there?

Don't you know there's going to be a statue? I myself have applied from the Panchayat. Set the statue in those grounds. We'll clear the wilderness with village *labour*.

You'll cut the fig tree?

No, Pishi, can such a large tree be cut? So many trees in these grounds. These tamarind trees will be sold. Also the jackfruit tree. They don't bear fruit. The money will go for the work of the Panchayat.

There'll be a statue if you say so?

Nothing comes of just saying, Pishi. The lady will dance only if you burn a lot of midnight oil.

The tree felling went on for a few days. Contractors came from town and bought all the mango, jackfruit, tamarind trees that didn't bear fruit. They all took a lot of kindling. They burned dried leaves to take the damp off the grounds.

Then a few days went in weeding, watering and levelling the ruined foundation of the house, and in general sprucing up. Dasu Soren told Nabin, *Labour* given. Clean-up done. So look, we're 42 people, worked hard for over a week.

If there's a road, you'll get back the cost of your *labour*. You'll get double what you didn't get now.

Will there be a road?

That's what they've said. PWD *sanction* has come.

Where will the statue sit?

There.

On what?

There will be a dais.

That's a job for construction workers.

Government will do it.

Government?

Let's see, let me go to *town*.

Sadan was full of hot air. It's our country's pride Nabin, our country's glory. You poor villagers did so much, I'll have the dais built. Let me find out how big a dais, I'll send the workers.

Did you find out about the road? When will they start?

I don't know yet, have you heard?

I've only heard that the MLA said everything will be done.

Then all's well. It's Patke's gain, Kannati's gain and Kandor's gain if there is a road in Chhatim.

That's what I'm saying. What's it to me if there's a road! You have a fertilizer farm in Patke, you have a small warehouse, you pull your goods by bullock-cart, now there'll be trucks. I have no business, no trade. When the road's finished I'll have wheat and peanuts grown in the village.

Very good, very good. Peanuts are a *cash crop* and wheat will grow well there.

I'll reconstruct our ruined tank with village *labour*.

That's a very good idea. Really, Nabin, I say from my heart, even to see that you think of others, work for others, pleases me. And see what evil inclinations I have? My father did the work and left all this, and I'm making it more and more.

Nabin goes to the house of the *MLA*. The *MLA* says—of course there will be a road.

He instantly becomes a campaign platform speaker and harangues Nabin, What do you mean there won't be? All the progress will be elsewhere? Chhatim, Dinu Thakur's village, will remain in darkness? There has to be a road. By that road the labouring masses of the village will travel to the outside world with the goods produced by their sweat, and come back smiling to the village with the wealth gained from their labour.

Nabin realizes that Babu is in full *flow* and it's not right to admit impediments in the way of the stream. Then, after the necessary pause, he says, I worked very hard for you before the election. I also worked before the Panchayat. I don't want anything for myself.

Then why are you a *press* apprentice? No peace at home?

Not at all Sir, just learning the work. Look Sir, we suffer a lot in emergencies—disease and accident—because there is no road here. If there is a road . . . the fire department goes to Temukhi village only because there is a road. The *ambulance* goes there from *town*.

True, but that village is close to *town*, after all?

Yes, we know Chhatim is far from any *town*. We don't hope that fire trucks and *ambulances* will go to Chhatim, that can't be. But if there's a road . . .

I know, I know. You don't have to explain the need for a road to me. But . . .

What?

If another village puts in a *claim* . . . ?

What's this you're saying now? I've been coming and going non-stop for three years for this road. And some other village—?

Well . . . you know . . . our MP, our Member of Parliament . . .

He knows, too.

See how some MPs have transformed their constituencies with roads and transport.

Let's see what happens.

Murari-babu at the press hears everything from Nabin. He's a born pessimist. He says, Since there's so much talk, there'll be no road.

No, no, there will. I've been trying so hard for so long and there'll be no road? Come on!

So you're trying, do you know if others are too? Even if they don't, then how many thousands will you pour on this area before you shell out for a road.

How many thousands for what?

Nabin, you talk like an idiot. How do you think the statue will come? By truck. Covered truck? How will all the functionaries and officers, the big fish and the small fish come? By road? Where's the road? You'll have to build a makeshift road for now. From the *highway* your village is through some green fields, some stony fields, some rice fields and Karnabati's dead river-bed. So won't you need money to build that unpaved road?

If I give *free labour* for that road? We won't need much building material, after all.

Don't get into that. Listen, I wasn't born yesterday. I know ev—erything that goes on. It's a PWD hassle, let PWD do it. I tell you what—go and tell that MLA Bhushno, let the labour come from the village. Let the villagers get a bit of cash.

All right.

This is a *town*, not a city. But Nabin is weary of these hundred twists and turns of the town's way of thinking. After all the necessary discussion he comes home.

Difference of opinion in the village as well. In his own family.

Sadananda says, Nabin, you're mad about this road, but have you thought of the consequences?

What consequences?

What's going to happen if there's a road?

You know it too, Baba.

What progress will happen—tell me that. You go back and forth to the *town*, what progress do you see, tell me? Our village ways are still decent. The girls don't wear *nylon*. The kids don't walk about with *transistors* pressed to their ears. Every place now full of mischief, and so poverty rises.

Let that be, Baba.

I know these words are poison to you, my son. But still I say, where do you see any good? It's all where's the next meal coming from, and pain and lamentation. What solution will getting the road be? Flood water will come in from outside. Will anything good happen?

Why not, let's see?

The only gain is that I won't get field hands, men to help with the thatch over our heads. Every mother's son will either leave or say give us outside rates.

If you can you'll give, otherwise not. If you can't afford more than eight-anna wages and a handful of rice, don't. So shouldn't they go elsewhere if they get a few pice more? They'll remain bonded to you?

You'll say that, sure. You have no feeling for the land.

True, I don't. Who benefited from this land of yours, this kingdom?

You're eating the rice grown on that land.

Suddenly Nabin gives a hard smile. I have the same right as you, he said. This is temple land.

I see! Who gave you this information?

She who can.

That witch?

She, too, has the same lifetime rights. That witch had an ounce-and-a-half worth of gold as her bride-wealth. That, too, has gone into your household.

Nabin, leave what you don't know . . .

I don't need to know. You stay right here with your reckoning. It's people like you who keep the village in such shape, can such a frog in a well survive today? If you'd had a road, Baba, your third son wouldn't have died of pneumonia at six years. We would've taken him to the hospital right away.

We could've. If hospitals and doctor's medicine cured everything, the *town*sfolk wouldn't ever have died. You, too, will die Nabin. You'll die trying to be better than others. Didn't Dinu Thakur die?

What names are you saying in the same breath, Baba? He and I? You can compare?

Sadananda suddenly loses his temper and says, If there's a sun and a moon I curse you, there will be no road, no road, no road. My son's a *leader* now! Such a saint outside, yet no respect for his father?

Keep up the food supplies to Pishi in right measure. I'll make a big problem otherwise. Don't forget! I'll stop your sowing and your reaping. I'll see who works on your land if I say 'no'!

Sadananda is now worried and says no more. His sister should say nothing about Dinu Thakur's statue. He wanted to tell Nabin this. He didn't. If Nabin's good he's good, if bad he's bad. What's more, all the villagers dislike

Sadananda and his youngest son. Nabin is their own. He shouldn't bother him and do himself harm.

At night Nabin's mother said, Why should you tell Nabin? Go once on the quiet and visit the old woman, threaten her.

I'll go to her room?

What's the problem if you stand in the door frame? Look, the god has no god-muscle these days. It was through her that we lost our worship practice, the priest was displaced. Wasn't the brahman's son hanged? Yet she wanders in the wilderness and the goddess's familiar, the python, doesn't bite her? So many people die of snake-bite, was she born with the gift of life forever? And she made my son a stranger.

You're quite right. I'll stand on the threshold and tell her everything. And what he said about her food supply . . .

Don't I give her stuff? Does she live on nothing, or can she?

Nabin is so single-minded . . .

He's got too stubborn.

With or without reason a human being can some-times be punch-drunk with the strangest bliss. If your head is constantly buzzing and dim due to eating too lit-tle for a long time, then such *euphoria* can easily attack you.

Such is her condition. Dinu's statue will stand in the village—the new look of the Thakur compound—the easiest conclusion from all this is that the village is grad-uating into modern times. Reaching the present from the past. Result—the dreamy drunkenness in her mind. Her head is in such a state from eating little, that it often seems to her that she's floating rather than walking. Now she often stands in front of the Thakur house. She fills her eyes with the shiny smooth broad plot of earth. A cactus fence all around. She looks and looks, and then returns.

She doesn't feel like cooking every day when she gets to her room. She eats a little chickpea powder and lies down. She strokes the piece of cloth that Nabin bought. She'll put it on the day Dinu returns to the compound. Nabin has said that it's the road rather than the statue that will be the true memorial to Dinu Thakur, that will show him respect in the proper way. Once he, too, had wanted to change his own times. The village has remained in the same shape from his time to this day. All will change if there's a road. That will be to show him real reverence. In Nabin's opinion, building a statue is secondary. The road is the real thing. Today these words are also her words. She doesn't know since when Nabin has become as necessary to her as Dinu, in another shape.

The road will be called Shahid Dindayal Thakur Road, Nabin has said. If there's a road little by little there will be a school, a *health centre*, all kinds of things in the village. The school will be called Dindayal Memorial School.

She laughs a lot. Affectionately. In her toothless face, with her skeletal frame, pebble white hair, on her fore-head and cheeks ringed with a million wrinkles, through her eyes of profound loving kindness, that smile is as exquisite as it is affecting. Nabin's heartstrings tear in pain. Pishi is like neglected soil. She looks cracked and dry like thirsty neglected soil. She still doesn't know how to complain. Just as thirsty soil, begging love, dresses itself in grass with just a bit of water, Pishi too wants to pour herself out with just a little love from Nabin. Always a smiling face, as if Pishi has acquired a king's ransom.

Daughter of a royal line after all! Dasu Soren, Ratan barber, Sadan Khan, Murari-babu—they all say from their childhood memories of the Manosha fair, that Pishi had been very beautiful. She looked like the daughter of a divine house. How she walked about! No one ever could say a bad word. Whatever happened, happened by the turn of the wheel of fortune.

Nabin loves Pishi even more. Unlike Baba, Pishi never holds out her hand for the smell of the pure butter of yesteryear. It's Pishi who's correct. Pishi says, What there was in the old days, not even Grandfather or Great-grandfather ever saw, why me? Yes, I saw land, but many people had land like that then. Dinu's sister was married into the Misra family of Patke. The Misras had much more land.

If Nabin is ever a wage-earner he'll make Pishi lie in a soft bed, wear whole cloth, eat food cooked by himself. He'll rub oil into her cracked hands, give her oil to put in her hair. He'll light a paraffin lantern in her room. For that long ago event, that caste-duty crossfire, they ruined Pishi's life. So many lives were torn apart. Why is the Thakur family extinct? Because a brahman boy loved a Bhunya girl? Such marriages happen all over the place these days. Does any one worry about this any more?

Nabin flares up with rage when he sees Pishi. Pishi complains about nothing. Pishi came only to endure. It's as if even the evil treatment she received at the hands of Nabin's father and brother was her due. How did it all fall due for Pishi? By whose judgement?

She's never known how many thoughts Nabin has on her behalf. Rapt in her own thoughts she returns home at evening. She has no clue how she looks. Like the village-goddess, the spirit of the village. As if she wanders asking and asking for a bit of attention, affection, compassion from the community. The village, too, is ageing. Getting exhausted.

Her sparse hair flies in the wind.

When Sadananda first stood in front of her room, at first she couldn't believe it.

Sister.

Who's there?

It's Sada.

Sada?

Sadananda. Nabin's father.

Is anything wrong with Nabin?

No. Come here for a minute.

You . . . you . . . whatever you have to say, say it from there. I can hear.

Dinu Thakur's statue is going up.

I know.

You should know first. There's Nabin! However. What I have to say is, fine, there's a statue. Whatever happens, happens. But you won't show yourself. Not a word to anyone.

What can I say?

Whatever happened, happened then. All the disaster came from you. Thakur-uncle threw away the house-worship, did not take the image even when Father begged on his hands and knees on bare earth. The line perished because of divine ire. We could no longer hold our head high. D'you remember all that?

Yes.

Don't you say any of that. Reporters might come. It's no use raking up old scandal. If you try to say anything, remember you'll have to get out.

Sadananda left. She sat like a stone. Again those memories, talk about the past. She closed the door like an automaton. Poured herself some water to drink. Then she climbed the platform and lay down.

5

What happened in 1924 was a many-layered *tragedy*. Multiple destructions with one explosion. The explosion was caused by Dinu and his tempestuous unrequited love. And later that became important. For example, Dinu's hanging—police violence in the Thakur house—after which violence the conflict between Mahananda and Dinu's father.

The priest returned the worshipped and-to-be worshipped image. Thus did the curse descend upon her life. The event was quite unthinkable for those days. Even killing the daughter through whom such disaster came would not have satisfied Mahananda.

Remembered, all is remembered.

After Dinu's departure Thakur-uncle's appearance is that of a lightning-struck coconut palm. He was enraged even by the Bhunya name. Yet he is the priest of the instated Manosha. He cannot say 'no'. Apparently he asked the sculpted five-snake-headed Manosha on the brass pitcher constantly, Did I neglect any detail of your service? Any detail?

Mahananda would say in private, This happened to him by the god's rage. He must have erred somewhere. This god is most ruthless. If there is error the consequence will be a curse.

Then came that fearful, fearful day. The news of Dinu's hanging. The entire village is in the courtyard of the Thakur house. Thakur-uncle enters the shrine-room, holds up the worship-scrolls and the brass image of the goddess, above his head. Then with tearless lamentations he tears the air and says, Mother, we worshipped you for a few generations, and you took my son as sacrifice? I will not serve you with these hands.

The god belonged to the Bhunya family. At that time Mahananda's brother's wife had had a daughter, the household was in the uncleansed ritual period of a birthing. Manosha being an exceedingly short-tempered goddess, she had to be taken to the Thakur house for any excuse at all.

Thakur-uncle says, I will not serve, and runs towardsto the Bhunya house holding the goddess on his head. He keeps shouting—Mahananda! Mahananda!

Mahananda runs out of the house. Sees that the priest is running to him with the goddess on his head. Up to now he, too, was stunned by the violence of the blow of Dinu's hanging. Now, seeing the priest enter the environs he forgets about Dinu and screams—Uncleansed! Uncleansed! Don't bring the god!—and immediately realizes that if he is in the birth-uncleansed period, the priest has sinned greatly by touching the god when unclean by death in the family. Manosha can't be kept clean any more. The moment this springs to his mind, before it can end, Thakur-uncle enters. Dulali has turned to stone. She stands holding the lintel. She sees it all.

Thakur-uncle is throwing the scrolls out into the courtyard, throwing the image. I return the god, he says, I return the shrine-room. You fed my son through that daughter of yours. I won't worship your god, I won't stay on your land. I curse you, let your line die, die, die.

You dropped the god of my line on the unclean yard?

Wasn't the eldest son of the line hanged by an untouchable?

You can't do this.

I just did it.

Don't make me a sinner, brother, don't become a sinner. Where will I go if you throw away the god?

Everything is so sunk in sin, Mahananda, you and I are not going to be saved by worshipping our god.

Brother!

No.

Holding his sacred thread, he runs saying, No, no, no. Mahananda falls to the ground and howls weeping. Holds up the Manosha pitcher and cries, Threw you away, Mother? Threw away?

His eyes fall upon his daughter. Murderer! he says and then swoons. The eldest son Shyamananda picks up the god, the pitcher, and the scrolls. The women of the Bhunya house also raise their voices in lament. These are the memories of a terrible, terrible disaster.

Mahananda keeps going to Thakur-uncle, keeps going. Thakur-uncle doesn't let him in.

Then one day the police come. The scene of the police coming across the Karnabati river-bed is seen first by the fisherfolk of this village, they leave their huts, run into the forest. An elephant comes behind. The landowners of Patke use the elephant to demolish the houses and barns of the tenants.

The police and the elephant come directly towards the Thakur house. Unverified *report*: Badan Khan points out the Thakur house and hides in the woods on the low hills by the Karnabati stream and, when the police create great violence, he walks by the stream a bit, climbs up, and escapes to Patke. Apparently he had *nagra* shoes[18] on his feet.

Then, amazing everyone, the Inspector drags out Dinu's unconscious mother, and the old female servant with his two-year-old sister in her arms. He drags out and throws to the ground Dinu's younger brother, and Thakur-uncle. Uncle falls on his face and when he stands you can see blood coursing down his forehead. A bloody sacred thread down his fair form. Mahananda runs forward, pushing all the villagers aside, all others with them. Thakur-uncle raises his hand and says, Keep off. Don't touch. I'm impure.

He lifts up his wife, his children, the old servants. Don't you weep, anyone. Anyone weeps, I'll behead them. It's a time to look, look on.

The trained elephant demolishes the structures at the mahout's goad. Pots and pans, rope-strung clothes-racks, cowrie-strung wall-brackets, bed, low-table, image-idol, rice basket, lentil-urn.

Mahananda runs up to say something to the Inspector, but Thakur-uncle says, Say nothing. Let it all go, let it.

Fire drops on thatch. Into the paddy stack. New straw and the autumn harvest burn merrily. The villagers

18 Shoes of local make, worn by the well-off.

can't bear it any more. Who is punished for whose guilt, they cry and they mourn.

Then Thakur-uncle kneels in front of the Inspector, saying Son gone, house gone. Please, walk your elephant over me, I beg you.

The Inspector is leaving with his group, he has left. The Inspector is turning around and saying, I am a servant of the Crown, I have to do shit-eating work, please forgive me.

Thakur-uncle is motionless under the tree with his hand on his forehead. He just stands there. Mahananda lies prone on the ground holding his feet. Rubbing his forehead on the brahman's feet. Saying, Take the god back, Brother. I will raise a new roof right away. I will give new land. Great harm will come to me, Brother. It has never happened that a priest has thrown away the image.

Why? She can throw me away, and I can't? She can light a living pyre in my chest, and I can't throw her away?

Gods can curse humans without reason, when has a human thrown away a god?

I have shown the way. Am I still a brahman, that I'll conduct a worship service? An untouchable hanged my Dinu, an untouchable lit his corpse, where is the brahman in me? Constable-police manhandled my wife in front of you? They pulled me to the ground, the divine couple, Radhakrishna's little shrine throne swam in elephant piss. Does a brahman remain a brahman after that? Does he? Tell me yourself.'

Great harm will come to me, Brother. I hold your feet and eat dirt, I eat dirt, Brother, take back the god, don't make a sinner of me.

Thakur-uncle's eyes dance with a terrible joy. He understands that to refuse the god will be to give the greatest blow to Mahananda. He says in a stern, harsh, rough voice, Your daughter is alive, Mahananda, after all. You have not known the loss of a child, and so you wonder what disaster can come to you. Why should I take your god? I wish you harm. I do. If this brings you harm, it will bring me peace, however minute. You brought so much harm to me through your daughter?

All is recalled. Will be recalled. Dulali is poison in the Thakur house, for Dinu's death. In this family Dulali is poison, for the divine rage, brahman's rage. Sadananda came and reminded her of all this after such a long while.

6

The dais was built, spacious, lofty. Engraved below:

Dindayal Thakur, martyred freedom fighter
(1900–1924)
He who gives life to the last drop, cannot,
will not, perish.

Some confusion arises as to whether the passage should run 'he who gives' or 'who gives'. Since neither of the Tagore anthologies *Chayanika* or *Sanchaita* was immediately available, this could not be *checked*.

The dais was there. Then a most temporary unpaved road. Sadananda asked Nabin, Is this your Dindayal Road?

No. This is for *jeeps* and *trucks*.

The government will kiss goodbye with this road alone.

Let's see.

Then what about *electricity*?

Might come.

The village will go to hell because of you. Once it was your Pishi. Now it's you.

I'm letting you get away with it. If I had heard Pishi's name in your younger son's mouth, I would have crushed his face.

Why not crush your father's face?

Don't think I don't feel like it.

Nabin says such things often these days. Sadananda provokes such words. The father feels a certain pleasure and the son a certain resentment at being fooled.

Sadananda can't remain quiet after this. Trucks will break down, Nabin, he says. The statue will not reach the village.

That would please you, but it won't happen. The police are accompanying the statue, they will guard it, bring it carefully.

Police!

Of course. The Minister will unveil the statue.

Police! Minister! So much nonsense around a village priest's son, penniless brahman stock, who became an armed robber, and went to the gallows!

You're the one who needs the road, Baba. When the road's done I'll show you the world. You'll see that there's a world outside the kingdom of the Bhunyas.

Yes, yes, I know, how many people have the sword and charter of Mansingh at home?

There are factories, wheat growing on arable land, outcaste doms and chandals going to school and college, there are other things to see. Charter and sword? If you search this very Midnapore district you'll find a thousand such charters and swords.

Nabin moves off to Pishi's room so that his father notices. So that his father hears, he shouts, Keep the red lentils, the potatoes, and the onion, Pishi. Boil up everything together. I'll eat with you today.

Nabin's mother bows weeping before the sacred pitcher. Sadananda says, Dinu's father left you and insulted you so, have you lost your powers in this latter age, Mother? Dinu's statue will be set up in the village, and you can't do anything about it?

The brass Manosha, with her wide-open indifferent brass pop-eyes, has been hearing the prayers of devotees for 200 years. She hears them still.

Nothing happens with Sadananda's prayers. The statue-inauguration day approaches. Finally one day the inhabitants of Chhatim and the other seven villages stand in line on both sides of the dirt road. Bronze-hard Dindayal Thakur returns home 54 years after his death, riding a Public Works Department (*Roadways*) *truck*. The long forgotten and suddenly rediscovered martyr is raised to the dais bound in rope much tougher than the hangman's. The square pedestal under his feet is placed in the basin of the dais and stabilized with poured *concrete*. The *school magazine photo* supplied by Sadan Khan was not very credible. As a result Dinu's hard energetic air, his astonishingly bright eyes are transformed into a new Dinu with a calm serious detached gaze. Dinu's statue, with its neatly folded hair on both sides of a cut parting, a tunic on its body, a dhoti around its waist and legs, a cotton scarf on its shoulder, is relieved to see from on high that the village has remained as sunk in the darkness of ignorance, poverty and underdevelopment as he had left it. Then the statue is wrapped in *cellophane*.

The police light a portable gas lamp and guard the statue. They have strict orders, so they cook and eat the staples they've brought along and sleep in the *truck* in shifts.

The next morning droves of jeeps keep coming as soon as it's 10 o'clock. Under the huge marquee put up by Nabin and his group, and paid for by the money of the Panchayat, are placed dhurries[19] and chairs given by Sadan Khan. The students of Patke School come to sing the national anthem. No fault can be found with the event—*reporter, mike*, garlands for statue and minister, tea and sweets for the guests.

Nabin says, Aren't you coming Pishi?

She says, No Nabin, I beg of you.

Why not?

I'll take a look at it later.

Are you crying?

Won't I cry? That day they beat and chased him off like a mad dog . . . his forehead was cut . . . today you, with so much respect . . .

Nabin leaves. Nabin must admit that his role had always been minor in the entire thing. Today's event, too, is externally arranged and controlled. Neither reporter nor government functionary pays any attention to him. *MLA* and Minister are talking to him. But that is in the interest of keeping up mass contact.

First there is a speech inside the marquee. Nabin greets the Minister, Sadan Khan, and invites them to their *chairs*. Other important guests take their seats.

19 Woven cotton rugs.

The singers are on the dhurrie in front. The villagers overflow the dhurrie on all sides. Sadananda is noticeably absent. Ratan barber's thin, pot-bellied, eight-year-old daughter Mira, wearing a cheap pink nylon dress and a ribbon around her hair glistening with oil, garlands the Minister, Sadan Khan and the *MLA*. Consequently the *officer* from *PWD Roads* gets no garland.

Next the Minister, the *MLA*, and Sadan Khan give long speeches about Dinu Thakur. In closing Nabin is asked to say something. When, after thanking his audience, Nabin says, Now, thanks to their generosity we're getting a road, Martyr Dinu Thakur Road . . . then suddenly the *MLA* pulls his *shirt*. He pulls Nabin down into a chair and says, I, too, am interested in building a road. But currently the government is moving through a variety of obstacles. Therefore the road cannot be brought within the purview of a particular scheme. It is necessary that this road be built and I'm submitting a request to our distinguished Minister to consider this road under some future plan.

Forgetting protocol Nabin shouts, You've promised a road, a *school*, a weekly market, a *health centre*.

Don't put the cart before the horse, Nabin. Let the government be stable, everything will follow.

Now it's proven that Nabin is a rural boy. He does not have the militancy and ready wit of the town. For his eyes fill with tears and he weeps loudly. He doesn't even think of asking the villagers to surround the Minister and extract a promise by chanting: What do we want? A road. When do we want it? Now.

Murari-babu from *town* and Ratan barber from the village hold his two hands and say, Nabin! Let's do the task at hand now. Can work be done so easily? Do they care? We'll see. If not today, tomorrow.

Nabin frees his hands and says to the Minister, You know, when Dinu Thakur left the village, there was no *school*, no road, and we lit our lamps with mahua-fruit oil. There still is nothing in the village, the difference being we light paraffin. Just a road. If that can't be arranged . . .

I'll keep it in mind.

All rise and the Minister says to Sadan Khan, It's true about the road. But that you, too . . .

For us it's more important to have a statue of Dinu Thakur, Sadan says. Otherwise Bhushan would not have asked for it.

Of course. The village martyr. The nation's pride. And the statue is impressive.

The Minister climbs the dais and opens the covering. Cameras click. Then suddenly the Patke schoolchildren start the national anthem.

Nabin moves to the thin stream of the river. He can't stop his tears, the 'hail and triumph' of the refrain of the anthem, in raised childish voices, pursue him.

The whole day passes. Nabin lies clasping his pishi all day. And all day Pishi strokes his body, his head, and consoles him.

I'll go away to town with you. Murari-babu says the Press will let us stay.

Your Panchayat?

I'll come here and do the work.

Do that.

You'll come, no?

Sure. I've nothing to worry about if I go with you.

Here you eat half a bellyful alone, there we'll both half-starve.

All right.

Murari-babu says he's old and can't keep everything under control. I'll look after the *Press*. A lot of work there. I, too, will work on *commission* basis.

All right. Your father?

I won't eat their food any more.

Dusk falls. Then Nabin sees. Pishi is putting on a clean cloth, combing her hair, wrapping herself in the shawl Nabin had given her.

What's up?

Get up.

Why?

Don't I get to have a look?

They didn't want to see you at all?

What did you expect?

They talked so much, did they know him?

Those are the ones that speak. Your father sees you as bad, calls you bad names, does he really know you?

In all that day, Nabin was more deeply consoled by these few words than by the hundred assurances offered by Murari-babu. The villagers had told him, The thing didn't get done by your words, but we haven't lost faith in you. Still, Nabin hasn't been able to get over his shame. As their spokesman he could get nothing done. His mind says, if I'm Nabin Bhunya, I'll get a road made. Yet pain and sorrow—can one lose the pain of disappointment so easily?

Nabin took the flashlight. They stepped out of the room. Pishi stood before the statue. Slowly raised her face. Nabin shone his flashlight.

So big! So high! You can see the sky behind him.

Nabin now sees with Pishi's eyes. Very big, very high. In the dark, at night. Human pain and compassion in the bronze eyes.

He is looking at us, look Nabin!

Yes.

Pishi looks her fill. Goes forward. Passes her hands over the statue's feet. A strange, unknown feeling. Why can she not match this high, great statue with that Dinu? Has Dinu become a god? Like the open shrine of Manosha?

Pishi, you'll catch a cold.

Yes, let's go.

Suddenly Pishi surprised him and said in a voice of tearless dry pain, The flowers at his feet are already wilted, Nabin. Crows will shit on his head, dirt will cover him, haven't you seen the distress of the god at Manosha's open shrine all year round?

Drawing Pishi close with great care, holding her hand, walking towards her room, Nabin says, They spent 74,851 rupees for the statue—the dirt road—the *function*. They could have gold-plated the village with that money Pishi, they would have got road, *health centre*, *school*, ev—erything. The living are dead and yet . . .

The statue behind them stands in the same glory. It's not Dinu, it's a statue. Setting up—establishing—inauguration—subsequent neglect—a statue has nothing to do with this. Yet for the sake of a statue a great disappointment can descend on the Nabins of this world, it has happened to this Nabin.

Nabin and Pishi keep walking in the dark.

The Fairy Tale of Mohanpur

OLD ANDI ALONE KNOWS the fairy tale of Mohanpur. In which fairy tale there are paddy stacks in every house, and cows in every cowshed. In that fairy tale Behula is a flowing river. Whenever the fisherman casts his net in that river, silvery fish come up as the harvest of the water.

In that fairy tale there is no starvation, no famine, no despotism from Hedo Naskar, none of the unbearable suffering of the sharecropper, no disease, no decrepitude.

Old Andi hasn't seen the Mohanpur of fairy tale with her own eyes. Her ancestors hadn't either. That Mohanpur did not exist in reality. When Behula changed its course, it went under water. Yet another Mohanpur has come to be.

In this our Mohanpur, the poverty is complete. Irkanpur Station is two hours by train from Calcutta. If you go east from the station you find the village of Behula. After a little ways east you must veer south. You find the village of Mohanpur if you walk three miles. It's a village of fishers and Tior-Kaot outcastes.[1] All paths are walkways criss-crossing Naskar's paddy fields.

Old Andi's waist has fallen. Her eyesight is dim. All day she picks the bitter thankuni herb, the fruit of the fig, the auspicious durba grass, she scrapes the surface of the muck-choked pond to get land snails to give to Durga, to Batashi in the fishers' quarters. In the small hours they run along the aal—the raised path criss-crossing the paddy—and catch the Calcutta train. They return in the afternoon and settle with Andi. They subtract their own share.

Durga says, With four sons why kill yourself slaving?

Andi says, Belly's sake. Do they say, Ma, why do you sweat? They do what they can. Bad times. Really bad. Whatever they bring goes to buy rice.

And where is this rice? All the rice travels to Calcutta. Folk sieve rice night and day.

You call this justice? Can landsfolk buy rice at nine rupees a kilo?

Listen, Mashi,[2] we'll always have bad times. Hang back and forth on the train day in and day out, with five rupees tucked in at the waist. And to feed your face with that? With seven mouths to feed.

Wasn't like this before. I close my eyes and see your Pishi Anna cooking a lot of stuff for the puja-feast.

Don't go on with that. It's because the aunts cooked so much back then that there's nothing left for us. How did Calcutta folk live then, say? Now you sweep the village clean and send all the rice, all the greens.

I shut my eyes and see everything clear as clear. I open my eyes and it's dark.

---

1 Amongst the lowest of the low castes.
2 Mother's sister.

Bad times, bad times. You can see only with eyes shut now. Mashi, shut your eyes and look at food to eat, cloth to wear, oil for hair, ricks of paddy-straw.

I see everything dimly, dimly child. Why's this?

Batashi is still silly. Ask your grandson to take you to Irkanpur. See a doctor, get medicine, you'll see better, she says.

Durga's the *realist*. When to go, if she's chasing Boss's cattle all day? she asks. How you do talk! Gie't a rest. Mashi? Eat boiled snails. Snail broth for dim sight. Remember the Kobrej-herbalist say that? To eat snails?

Desperate, Andi goes to pick snails and, wonder of wonders, finds a new variety of frisky, many-coloured eel. When she ties it in her thin-weave washcloth, her gamch-ha, and brings it home, her eldest daughter-in-law opens the bundle. She screams. The eel becomes a water-snake and escapes slithering.

Everyone scolds the old woman. You caught a snake alive? they ask.

You'll catch a water-adder one day and croak.

Eh! As long as there's the snake-doctor Chhire Mal in Behula I'll not die of snake-bite.

The youngest son speaks unwelcome truths. By the time you get to Behula and catch Chhire you'll be dead and gone to hell.

What? I'll go to hell? You dare so high?

Sure I dare. Such greed to eat fish!

I'd not have eaten alone!

No, you'd share. Hey, is there fish in our future that we'll eat fish? Scrape the canals and creeks and get the lit-tle fish, that's our hope. If we lust after big fish, it'll run off as a snake.

Hearing this, the eldest son Nada says, Why? Won't Gran bring a big fish if she gets one?

The youngest son says, Hey, you dung-beetle's son, you want us to be motherless out of greed for fish? Fish-eating! If there's a crop on low-lying land, if Naskar lets me bring the crop home, then I'll feed you big fish. I can't lose my mother for fish.

He reveals his filial affection by way of this grand declaration, feeds on fistfuls of cold gruel and goes to the field. The entire thing now graduates into a new version of a fairy tale. Andi says, astonished, I caught a fish and it became a snake?

The eldest daughter-in-law says, Why did you go?

To get snails.

Why?

I don't see clear, snails would have cut the dimness.

I'll bring you snails.

Do that.

Andi is overjoyed and says, If anyone'll bring, it's you. Who else looks out for me?

The shadow in Andi's eyes doesn't clear with snail broth, and one day, trying to pick thankuni, she falls into a mossy pond, mistaking it for a meadow. Her second grandson lifts her, and when she has recovered from her immersion Andi herself says, Everyone knows it goes like this. You say fish and it's a snake. You step in a meadow and it's a slime pond.

The youngest son says, Stop your fairy tale. You're going blind.

Then take me to the hospital.

How will you go?

Why, walking?

Why should the doctor look at you?

And why not?

Do they look at the poor?

Wait, let me tell Enayet.

Tell. Enayet opens his heart to the poor. Because the fucker has a government job.

Mussalman on top o'that, and a scholarship boy.

Go to him, then.

Enayet graduated from middle school and got a job as a *peon* in a hospital. He bribes the doctors and gets them to look at patients and his influence is strong in the village. He has sold about a 100 coconuts this year. Also bananas of the Agniswar variety. He's thrown out his thatch for a tin roof. For reasons of this kind he keeps everyone in the village happy. For the aristocratic appearance of his house looks ugly in the poor Muslim quarter. Like *lipstick* on the lips of a skeletal beggar girl. He doesn't want to take note of his neighbours' envy. It is just as factually true that he is upwardly mobile as it is that his neighbours might feel envious. By behaving well with everyone to the best of his ability he balances these two opposed realities.

It is to this Enayet that Andi goes. Says, Aw Enayet. I'm in trouble dear.

Tell me, Mashi.

Now you're my hope.

What is it?

I see blurred and dim in my eye.

Come to hospital with Nando.

Nando can't make time. Nando's son Nodo takes Andi. Andi has great good luck. In a bit they see Matiur's ox-cart.

Matiur says, Come along. How long will an old person walk, step by step?

Andi comes to the hospital sitting on straw. The Irkanpur Health Centre is unable to bear the health requirements of this Behula *Block*. The population of the Behula *Block* villages is 7,051. There are 20 beds at the Health Centre hospital, on the average there are 60 patients at any given time. It is a daily sight to see more than one patient to a bed, patients strewn on the floor.

Twenty *beds* cannot *justify* two doctors, this the doctor-in-charge grasped long ago. It is not possible for him alone to prescribe the procedure for the *malaria, cholera,* worms, blood dysentery, dropsy, tuberculosis—*typhoid, pneumonia, encephalitis*—anaemia, *diabetes, gastric ulcer,* cuts—body blows—burns—snake-bite, mad dog or fox-bite—ear infection—*diphtheria,* etc. that afflict the bodies of the average 100 outdoor and 60 indoor patients, debilitated and resistance-less as they are with malnutrition.

For medicine he gets the ingredients for a pink mixture—*enteroquinol, sulphadiazene, sulphaguanidine* and plenty of contraceptive pills—the situation is depressing. Because women are not enthusiastic about contraception here. The tip-top missies with family planning training who come here to explain the benefits of all that follows from the red triangle symbol of family planning get their ears bent in the following way:

What do you know? Our strength is in numbers. The more the better.

Pain? What pain? When a tree hurts to bear fruit, the world will topple.

What's it to you if I have 10?

The doctor knows that his situation is comparable to a fishing boat sunk under 14 feet of water. He will not get a *nurse-cum*-midwife. That work is done in Calcutta hospitals by trained just-adult females.

Where will they live here? There's no place to live. They can't come without brick buildings and safe residences. The Health Centre has no surrounding walls and is not secure. Armed robbery and larceny are *chronic* here. A lot of agitation has not produced a room for the nurse.

At the moment the doctor lives in terror, having received news of one particular governmental good wish. He, too, might obtain a *community health worker* with three months' *training*.

The aim is noble. These health workers will be let loose with some medicine, *bags* and a monthly allowance of 50 rupees. They will fill in the blank between the government health-plan and popular need.

The doctor feels that the implementation of the appointments will be on the basis of political reliability. Then those well-wishing youths will send even more patients in this direction.

The very thought makes the doctor feverish. If he were a doctor from Calcutta he could have escaped from time to time. He's from Sabudpur. He can escape no further than Sabudpur. He does—the patients drag him back from there as well.

It's the government that is the cause of the doctor's loss of heart. When the government *sanctioned* a cook for the Health Centre, it had no *kitchen*. Now there is a *kitchen*, but no cook.

Groceries are supplied by Hedo Naskar. The temporary cook takes a cut out of the supplies. The patients are happy with an *apology* for food!

There is never any disinfectant, cotton wool or *bandage*. In an *emergency* the doctor boils his instruments and lights a hurricane lantern to operate.

Why should it be a surprise that both the *compounder* Hari Nandi and the *peon* Enayet examine patients?

Knowing all, Enayet asks Andi to come. Andi and Nodo wait for a long time. Andi shakes her head constantly. This Health Centre seems to her an astonishing heaven. She says to her grandson, Great if I get in once. A bed to lie on, a belly full of food. Ouf, what a lot of convenience, Nodo.

Andi's call comes at about two in the afternoon. Andi had cleverly brought a bit of chickpea powder and a few molasses-balls in her waist cloth. Crushing it in her palm she's eaten that in little mouse-bites all this while. Otherwise she couldn't have waited hungry. Nodo had brought money. He went for tea and bread to the railway station.

The doctor understands nothing from Andi's eyes. He is not supposed to. He's not an ophthalmologist. There is no ophthalmological arrangement at the Health Centre. The first Saturday of the month an ophthalmologist, the second a dentist, the third a dermatologist—this arrangement still exists on paper. Our doctor has never seen those doctors.

Now, seeing a whitish spot on Andi's iris the doctor is immensely angry with Enayet. Do you play jokes on people, says the doctor.

Why?

Is there any arrangement for eye examinations here?

Take a little look.

Andi says in a pitiful voice, You won't show mercy? Aw, Doctor-babu. You're curing so many troubles of so many people and no mercy for me? Sitting here a—ll morning. And now the sun's moved all the way?

The doctor sighed. Yesterday he had the runs. He's doing his round since dawn till two in the afternoon on nothing but some parched rice soaked in water. He says nothing of himself. He looks into Andi's eyes carefully with a flashlight. Then he gives her a free sample of *eye-drops*, and 10 free samples of *multivitamin* tablets. Use these drops for your eyes, Old Mother, he says. And take these pills every morning for 10 days. Nothing can be done for the moment. In two months a lot of doctors will come here. Tents will be pitched, there will be eye *operations*, do you understand? Your eyes have cataracts, Old Mother.

That's why I see everything blurred?

Yes, Old Mother. Have to cut into the eyes. It can't be done now. In two months.

I'll be blind by then, my son?

No, no, cataracts can't be cut like a shot you know, Old Mother? A cataract is cut when it's ripe.

You'll take me into the hospital then, my son?

The doctor *humours* her, Of course.

Andi says with extreme anxiety, And then all my sickness will be cured, my son?

Why?

So much to eat?

The smile on Andi's toothless face pierces the doctor's heart like a spear. Goodbye for now.

Andi blesses him and leaves.

Returned home, her tales of the hospital are endless.

How the doctor looked with a light, gave her medicine. How he gave hope.

The youngest son says, Like a fairy tale?

It's like a story, ya!

With infinite gratitude she gives Enayet a little arum root when she picks a few from the yard to send to the market.

The eldest daughter-in-law says, If you'd sold it at the market we could have bought groceries? Doesn't he have arum roots in his own yard?

I planted those roots myself, says Andi. Just to give one! Without him who's going to get my cataract out?

Andi herself is deluded with her *eye-drops*. She thinks she sees everything clearly. Taking the pills, she thinks she feels stronger. She asks from time to time, Hey, Nodo, remember those two months? How much longer, eh?

It'll be when it is, Gran.

Is that an answer?

The eldest daughter-in-law sighs. Says, Ma, what does he know. I'll see that you get there when the time comes. How can he know?

Andi has profound faith in her eldest daughter-in-law, profound hope. If you say it'll be, it'll be, she says. Then she comes around and says, Hey, will you burn these ripe telakuchos?[3] Then I'd eat a little rice with some green chillies?

The second daughter-in-law says, You just ate!

I've ate? What a shame! I feel like I've eaten nothing. Give me a plate of puffed rice, then.

You'll eat puffed rice now?

Eldest daughter-in-law says, irritated, Does she have any sense any more, Kadu? Is there a difference between her and Meni's baby? The more you talk, there'll be more talk. Give her a handful of puffed rice. We still have to flatten 15 kilos of rice for parching.

Hey, daughter-in-law, give me a bit of parched rice?

Naskar's men will husk me with the rice-husker then. It's their order.

All that you flatten, everything?

All.

Why? They can't do it themselves?'

3 Creeper with red edible fruit.

Eldest daughter-in-law shakes her head sadly. Is it only Andi? Her mother-in-law. The entire household relies on her. That's why the eldest daughter-in-law begs Naskar-mistress and gets the job of flattening parched rice, frying puffed rice. And gets rice in exchange. High yield paddy gives heavy rice grains, it doesn't gain as much volume with boiling. It's still rice, though.

All four of Andi's sons plough Naskar's fields. In every village of the *Block* Naskar has land, Naskar has relatives. 'Ceiling' in landholding is a word made for rural Bengal. A state-run farce. The word 'ceiling' does not apply to people like Naskar. Naskar's land is everywhere. Others do the cropping. Although they farm the land, they're not sharecroppers. Naskar pays them according to his own convenience each year. In money and rice.

It's also not possible to say that this is illegal. Naskar is also the owner of the fisheries and the cold storage. He is the *order supplier* for everything at the Health Centre. On top of it all, he is the head of the Panchayat at the moment. In Mohanpur his first cousin Prananath looks after his property.

No one can circumvent Prananath to get something done in Mohanpur. Andi understands nothing. But Andi's sons are at present helpless before Prananath's eloquence. Prananath is threatening them. Do not join the sharecroppers' *union*, Nando. It'll be no good.

But Gobindo's group won't let go.

No good will come of it. Gobindo belongs to that group. Mango and milk will mingle, and the stone will be left high and dry.

As a result, Andi's sons now have a huge problem. When it comes to giving protection to the sharecroppers, Hedo and Gobindo belong to the same Party. In his own case Hedo refuses to obey any law. Gobindo is pure by nature and hot by temper. He does not understand short cuts. His verdict is clear. If Andi's sons are not included in the sharecroppers' *union* for fear of Hedo, then they, too, are Hedo's followers and saboteurs of the government's good intentions.

It is not possible for Andi's sons to explain to Gobindo that, in the village, Hedo Naskar is also *government*. His fields are tilled according to some audience-requested latest-hit programme, killing no snakes, and breaking no clubs, as the saying goes. None of Hedo's 150 tillers are ready to break that arrangement. Gobindo cannot understand that the apathy of these starvation-fearing broken-backed people is not *sabotage*; they haven't the skill to practice *sabotage*. Gobindo is proof of the sort of trouble that a well-intentioned dedicated activist can create for villagers.

For a few days Gobindo takes off for Calcutta. Andi's sons forget about him and sow rainy season paddy on Naskar's low-lying land.

After a while Gobindo reappears in the form of a *community* health worker in a luminous shape. Gobindo has always been a short-tempered honest person. He is honest in his devotion to the Party and also forthcoming with his shoulder if an uncle of a fellow-villager from the opposite Party suddenly dies. He is determined to observe celibacy and serve the masses under the *Party banner* all his life. He has not understood why the things he has done so far haven't done anyone any good.

He would grab boys and girls and send them to *primary school*. He would scold their guardians, They'll benefit tremendously if they learn to read and write, do you know that? If they remain dumb cattle like you they'll vote for the Congress Party, not the Communist Party (Marxist).

The guardians would say, It's these ignorant dumb cattle who *voted* for you. Didn't they, or are you forgetting?

So you did.

Well, you took our *votes*. And called people as old as your father dumb cattle. Well, God's given you good luck, so you say what you like. But why don't you give us some paraffin? Can we do without light? With snakes everywhere?

T'will come, t'will come.

Bring paraffin. Naskar has filled his house with *permit*-sanctioned paraffin.

Immediately Gobindo goes to Hedo Naskar. He has extracted paraffin by feeding him the necessary adjectives such as enemy of the *Party* in friend's clothing, and given the stuff to Mohanpur. He's been able to get the children to school only after doing all this, and trying to think about this, Gobindo has felt a pain in his chest.

It's good for them if their children are educated. He had to give paraffin to do this good deed? Degeneration, degeneration. No doubt the masses have suffered such moral degradation because of the Congress Party's misrule.

Even the school is empty. Students are learning how to work in the field with their fathers. Minding cattle. Gobindo was insulted when he tried to say something. Don't scold so, Gobindo, one old man said. How can you know if the result of book-learning is good or bad? Not even passed one exam, you.

Another was so contrary that he said, You passed one exam and so you've stayed a man, thinking of the poor. Our Prananath Naskar finished high school when he had two sons already, and now he swings a big stick on the poor.

Is that so? I'll see who gives you paraffin this time.

You will.

Why?

For us. Isn't it from the *gorment*?[4] If you won't give us *permit*-paraffin, why have we voted for you?

Gobindo has to work with people like this.

Then the sharecropper thing. Hedo Naskar's cheating you, Gobindo tried to explain. He's not acting right.

Then why have you made him Head?

You unite.

Why should we unite? Doesn't the *gorment* know what kind of man Naskar is? If he's to be let go, let the *gorment* do it. Are we going to get killed fighting and rioting against someone the *gorment* can't control?

I'll be here.

Naskar doesn't fear you.

He'll sure hear from me.

Son! Listen to an old man. You are a Patty boy. Naskar won't cross you. He'll appear to go along. But . . .

What is it, spit it out. Why cough with phlegm in your throat? Give it a honk, spit it out.

The speaker is an old man. Lifting his crusted yellowish eyes, filled with infinite kindly contempt he says, A sharecropper gets freehold in 12 years. Naskar was not in your Patty, now he's in tight. You know him, too. Naskar calls you to plough with a new thumbprint at 11 years. Whatever Patty he goes to, does he grant sharecroppers' rights? Does he ever give that much rice? Nothing will come of this, son, just the small folk will get crushed.

This can't be.

It has been, it is always, it is now, it will be, still you say it can't be. Why don't you understand what you see?

4 Government.

You make trouble with Naskar, he won't care for the Patty. Let it go.

This is unreasonable!

Gobindo! You would have been a father if you'd married. When you brought Naskar to the front, raised him up, didn't you know what his price was? Has he ever thought of others, that he will today? He got scared and ran off during the Naksali[5] days, and then he said the Naksalis are threatening me because I'm a Patty brother—so the last government gave him milk and honey, and so did you. Now why do you think he will suddenly think of others, become good? Whatever. Let Naskar be as he is. Our lot is not to be bettered. All around us people are getting their claims, their shares, and we'll just look on.

Gobindo understands the judiciousness of the old man's words. Suddenly he understands vaguely why, in spite of his own honesty and sincerity, Hedo Naskar is somehow still useful to the government. What do I know, he says. Where what is decided, we can't even know. However, let me make sure you get your paraffin.

Gobindo offers promises of this sort. And he no longer asks Andi's sons to leap into the sharecroppers' movement.

For a little while many questions arise in his mind. Then he is informed that he's been selected as a *community health worker*. Why him? Can the village carry on if he leaves the village? The villagers have entered the *system* of Gobindo's body and mind. He tells the villagers, I'm going to *Daiman Harbour*.[6] Then I'll go to Calcutta.

5 Naxalite; a member/supporter of the Communist Party of India (Marxist–Leninist), a militant revolutionary party.
6 Diamond Harbour, near Calcutta.

Why?

Can you run to the hospital each and every day?

No.

I'm going to learn the basics of treatment.

After? Be a doc?

Spoken like an idiot peasant. Is it easy to be a doc, I ask you? How much learning you have to have? How many years you have to study? How many thousands of rupees needed? And you need money to set up a doctor's office.

That you do.

You have seen me all my life. I'm Modhu Koiborto's son Gobindo. My father's a sharecropper. His son saw that and didn't learn to read and write. Someone's going to spend 20,000 rupees to make me a doc? Or do I myself have that money? My dad pushed me to school and I went to the field.

That I know.

Some old sorrow rises in Gobindo's breast. There was a time when I tended Naskar's cattle. My dad had no money, I didn't go to school. But I dreamed a lot of dreams as I came home on the back of a cow. I was a medico in my dream. I was an engineer. I was a train driver. Sometimes I was Naskar.

What you said last. That was not a good dream, we'd have died if there were two Naskars.

Later I started social work, Party work—I have no more pain. No, uncle, I'm not going to be a doc. I'll inoculate for smallpox, give cholera shots—look after minor wounds, cuts, burns—get patients into hospital. I'm going to learn that stuff. My worry is about you. Even with me around there's no end to your misfortunes. What will you do when I'm gone? I'm worried.

The villagers understand the sincerity behind his words. The village worker Gobindo is their only way of connecting with the incorporeal entity called government, ever-absent in rural life.

Even after grasping his sincerity, the thought that Gobindo might some day give them injections fills them with fear. Gobindo, after all! Maybe he'll catch 'em, tie 'em to the post of the stoop and put the needle in.

Adhar Koiborto sighs and says, Don't be quite out of sight, Gobindo. Then we'll get no wheat, no paraffin.

No, no, I'll surely come.

Gobindo keeps his word. After his training he'll get about 50 rupees a month *contingency* pay. Hearing this, his mother says instantly, Shall I look for a girl?—aw, Gobindo!

Why? Why look for a girl at all?

You'll be a doc, getting a 50-rupee job, start a family?

Family! In room and yard you want a gaggle of kids honking like small geese, eh? I'm not your son alone, now. I'm a Party worker, the public's.

The public will shit on your shoulder, ya. I ask you, you were made in my belly or the public's? You've lost your sense with your Pat—ty stuff?

You dare talk about the Pat—ty? says Gobindo and in blessed rage he slams down his bowl of cold rice, slams and breaks the wooden seat he was sitting on, and exits.

Mother looks at the younger brother's wife with wet eyes and says, What a thing the Pat—ty is, dear? My Gobindo has cooled his hot temper? Before he would have broken the clay stove with a bamboo pole?

Truly?

Ask your husband. Broke as many clay cooking pots as stoves. This is thanks to the Pat—ty. Otherwise I've given him talismans, bathed him in Chondi's shrine water, his temper's remained the same!

The younger daughter-in-law is a bit depressed. She had wanted to arrange a marriage between her first cousin and her elder brother-in-law.

Then Gobindo leaves the village for training. Naskar says to his own cohorts, The longer that jerk stays away, the better. A real butt-kicker, that boy. He only knows how to poke people to make them sore. Hey paraffin, ho wheat. If there is a stock of paraffin you can get it at time of need. Did one always have paraffin, or get it at will?

Who's to understand this?

In today's world everyone is hot-tempered. Gobindo says, give wheat. Did they ever know wheat or eat roti?[7]

Of course not!

Who's to hear?

These people who play half-full half-empty with Naskar let him know when Gobindo comes to the village. Gobindo says, Why here? Whyn't you go there and kiss arse?

The words that come to Gobindo now are his own, not approved by the Party. Son of a sharecropper. His reactions are like the villagers'. He arrives at Naskar's. And says, Here, Uncle. I'm here because it's time for *permitted* paraffin and the *rationed* allowance of wheat.

Wouldn't I have given, or don't you trust me, eh? If distrust enters among your own Gobindo, disaster is soon to follow.

Our hope is that you're around.

Why are the sons of Mohanpur's Andi hanging around? And I also see Chand, Haren and Shashodhar of your Koiborto neighbourhood.

7 Homemade bread, common staple in Indian homes.

I'm training them in this and that. You understand, Uncle? I'm becoming a health worker, you know. I won't be able to help you at all times. These people are here. How many things can you manage alone? Now it's the government rule. You must work together.

Right, right.

Naskar digests these body blows and decides that Gobindo must be taught a lesson as soon as posssible. All he says is, I'll do what you say. In the British days we called volunteer those who burnt corpses, put out fires. At the post-sacrifice dip in the Behula river, Chhire Mal's aunt drowned because there were no volunteers.

Why didn't the others swim?

But that's the volunteers' job!

Now we can't work that way, Uncle. We must go forward with what each of us knows.

To Naskar this is as bitter as neem.[8] Gobindo says, I can't think of Mohanpur alone. I'll take men from Beulo as well. They'll keep track of people, inspect cards, distribute things.

As you say.

I don't say for nothing. If people got things I'd make no noise. That I have to speak is the sad thing, d'ye see, Uncle?

Gobindo's face flushes as he speaks, the veins stand out on his forehead and Naskar remembers Gobindo's proverbial temper. He says in the smoothest voice, My son! I'm growing old, with a thousand tasks on my head. Don't I make mistakes? Forgive and forget. Do I myself know everything? You, too, will let me know.

Hearing this, Andi's son Nando laughs suddenly. Naskar sees that. Offended, he says, I spoke in good faith

8 Margosa tree, very bitter, with medicinal qualities.

and you laughed, Nando!? So laugh. God has brought the day when some must swallow kicks from frogs, and some launch the kicks.

Okay he has laughed, it was wrong, but as for now, you haven't been kicked and Nando hasn't kicked, Gobindo says. Tomorrow morning wheat/paraffin will be given out. This time I'll stand and oversee.

Whatever you say.

Gobindo comes out and says, Isn't that Chhire Mal? Aw, Uncle Chhire, where you off to?

To you. You're now playing hard to get. Can't get to see you.

I came to Behula village three hours ago. Where were you?

Where do you think! I heard that you beat Naskar up and got some wheat and paraffin?

No, no, I arranged for the distribution of permit goods. Why should I beat him up?

Sripad (nickname Chhire) Mal is a famous snake-bite doctor even outside of Behula village. He is a snake-bite shaman and he is also a being dedicated to his own profession. His mental outlook is fully scientific. He knows the limits of medical treatment and he accepts patients in hospital. Sripad is fighting for a long time against the absence of *snake venom antiserum* in the hospitals. Such is his personality that although as a Mal he depends upon medical treatment he still keeps people's respect. Sripad's face generally carries an air of quiet defeat. He knows that he is defeated in the matter of curing patients bitten by snakes. He has accepted his defeat.

Now his face does not show his habitual calmness. Rage. He says, The bastard is a great sinner.

What's the matter?

There, listen. Do you hear weeping?

Gobindo listens. Recognizable weeping. Spread all over ocean-girt rural India. A woman weeping with a corpse in front of her. This lament can be heard in all the languages recognized by the Indian Constitution, and in all the oral languages of aboriginals and tribals. In this sort of weeping there is usually verbal elaboration, and because the weeping is near, Gobindo can hear.

You asked me to cook arum greens when you left. I've cooked arum greens, dear!

Who's gone

Motaher. That's why no one from Behula was with you.

Strange, no one said anything?

What's the use of saying? Are there injishuns in the hospital? He left his family adrift.

When did it bite?

Morning. All because of that Naskar. That shit's son built a brick stack and flooded the village with snakes. You'll do a man's work, Gobindo, if you can break the stack by Naskar.

Gobindo gives a pained laugh. Says, Uncle Chhire! Madhu Koiborto's son can be in the Patty, he can give his life for you. But he can't have the brick stack broken by Naskar.

Can you have injishuns brought to the hospital?

Uncle, when you get injishuns, it has come thanks to Gobindo's care.

Can people live all year on that? Why doesn't a snake bite that bastard?

Sripad leaves, shaking his head. New anger against Naskar gathers in Gobindo's mind. As a result he comes the next day and gives everyone in Behula and Mohanpur wheat and paraffin in just measure. He says to them in Naskar's hearing, On the next date take just this weight and measure. The material will be here. If you don't get it let me know, arrangements will be made.

Then Gobindo leaves. Sripad tells him at the moment of departure, Cholera strikes rarely. Learn the snake injishun, why don't you?

I'll learn if they teach. You, the village heads, must take paraffin and wheat in just measure on permit day.

He'll give?

Don't talk like a stupid peasant, Uncle. It's your right, given by the government.

It's not right to abuse an old man while keeping Naskar in power, Gobindo.

If I've abused you, hit me back with your shoe. But take things in just measure nonetheless. I'll show him a thing or two if he refuses.

That's what I say. The government is giving, giving through your hands. And Gobindo is needed to get the goods out. What a state of affairs, eh?

What to do? This is what he's always done, he's always managed this way, so the habit has formed. His gut is bursting because he must change his habits.

Under every government Naskar ruled okay.

Today yes, but tomorrow?

Don't say that, Gobindo. Many people have said that through many administrations. Could they do anything?

Let's see.

After this Gobindo goes for training. He frequently checks out his own hunting-grounds. It's not easy to keep Naskar on the straight and narrow. Gobindo gives support to the villagers. But after the training period is over, Gobindo goes on *intensive training* with the other health workers in a fortnight.

It's after this that he returns luminously to Mohanpur with newly earned self-confidence. He has learnt the primary treatment of burn-cut-drowning. Learnt to inoculate for cholera and vaccinate for small-pox. Learnt to judge the symptoms of malaria.

As soon as he returns he does the rounds in Mohanpur and calls into Andi's house—O Andi Pishi! What's new in Mohanpur? Your Gobindo has come back learning doctoring, d'ye know that?

It takes him some time to understand that the bun-dle sitting on the stoop is Andi; when he understands, he receives a stiff *shock*, a blow to his senses. He has also learnt how to treat shock, but not all shocks can be treat-ed. Gobindo grasps that the *shock* he receives when he sees the fig-picking, thankuni-plucking, new-grass-culling, bent-over Andi Pishi as an inert bundle cannot be treated with *sal-volatile* or sugar-saturated water.

What's happened, Pishi?

Such is Gobindo's nature that he thinks on his own that Andi is reduced to this because he wasn't there. And he considers himself culpable.

Oh, Gobindo! What I went to do for good, turned bad, my son. My eyes . . . Andi howls weeping and Gobindo sees that the eyes shedding tears are bloody and addled. You cannot tell the iris from the whites. The most terrible thing is something like a bloodied and confused rage in those two eyes.

What's the matter? Eldest daughter-in-law comes forward with her cowdung-spattered hands. Hasn't the doctor told you not to cry? She scolds her mother-in-law. You mustn't cry at all.

Mustn't cry? Mustn't I cry when I have no eyes?

Mustn't cry. Here's Gobindo, he'll arrange every-thing.

Mustn't cry?

No. Didn't I tell you to wind me the string by measuring with your hands?

I can't do it, my love.

You can. Who says you are of no use? Then who is mixing cowdung and coaldust balls?

It is as if the daughter-in-law's words are magical. Andi wipes her eyes and winds the string. Water drips from her eyes. Gobindo looks at this, and the eldest daughter-in-law says with dry unease, Not weeping now. Her eyes drip if she weeps once.

What happened?

Eldest daughter-in-law speaks as she slaps the cowdung down into fuel patties, At the hospital they said there will be tents for eye-operation. There were. Enayet brought news. My brother-in-law and Nodo took her. They took a look and said, This is not cataract. A blood-vessel was torn in Mother's eye. They could've cut her eye if she weren't so old. They gave some medicine to put in the eye. They said the blurred vision would be there till she died. Her life would go on. When Mother made a big fuss they said, If we cut you even that little bit of sight will go.

How did it get like this?

Eldest daughter-in-law sighed. Batashi explained to Mother that someone sat in the Jabudpur market. Everybody's eyes are getting cured, they're giving glasses. When she said she'd go there her eldest son was cross. He said, Hospital doctor couldn't and this guy will cure your eye? You'll go blind. Don't even think of such a thing.

Then?

She went there in cahoots with Batashi. Didn't tell anyone at home, no one knew. Pran Naskar was stripping the coconut palm, suddenly she left saying, Let me go and tend cattle. I didn't know anything either. I had nearly three kilos of puffed rice to fry. Everyone breakfasted, and Ma left right away. There the person took two rupees. Whatever medicine he gave, Mother put in her eyes and started thrashing like a cut goat—saying 'Burns like mashed pepper, burns like mashed pepper.' Seeing this, Batashi brings her slung on her arms, comes running, you know?

Then?

I washed her eyes, fetched a bit of lotus-honey from the herbalist doctor's house, there's no one who practises herbal cures ever since the Master's death, well Mother-mistress gave a bit. Rubbed that in, covered her eye in a lotus leaf, went under water and got some mud from the pond-bottom and put it on the leaves, then it cooled down a bit. The next day we asked for an ox-cart and took her to Naskar's hospital. The doctor said that medicine had melted her irises. Nothing can be done about it. Gave some ointment. They said there's no cure here. A good doctor in Tamli. If he can do something. There's no cure here.

That man couldn't be caught?

Brother-in-law went to Jabudpur market two weeks running. No trace could be found.

All this falls on you now?

What to do? Throw her away? She brought me into this house at five years old, she would mind me with candy and sweet balls. That's her nature, to jump to every tune. Going to market on Batashi's word . . .

Gobindo says, Wait a second. Who will take this screw-loose body to Tamli?

But there's no way here?

Let's see. Send Nando to me.

Gobindo calls Nando and says, Now I know the rules. If he can't do it, he can call a doctor from the district town. Let him do that.

Pishi can't be taken to Tamli. Will he listen to you?

Let's see.

The doctor listens to Gobindo with infinite patience. Then he says, Do you know what she's got?

If I knew I'd be a doctor.

D'ye know diabetes? It's hard to *operate*. That's how the eye got infected.

Call a doctor from the district town. You have the regulations.

You will really have her treated?

You think I'm joking?

The doctor thinks for a bit. Then he says, By the rules I can ask for a doctor. Whether the doctor will come from the district town is not certain. I've asked twice and he hasn't come. The hospital at Tamli is good. Doctor Sarkar is a good doctor. Bring him on Sunday. I'll write a letter.

Why will the district town doctor not come?

Naskar-babu knows.

Hedo Naskar?

The doctor speaks in dry tones of deep despondency, The *tender* is his. Water for milk, rotten eggs for eggs, putrid fish, the sweepings of the warehouse for rice, and he has said a lot of things in the district town because I mentioned these things. I do not know how long I'll be here. He's trying to get another doctor.

Ask for the doctor.

Gobindo goes directly to Hedo Naskar. It is one of my duties to see that the hospital is working properly, he says.

How can it with such a doctor?

A bad doctor! Oh, you're good. Why then are you supplying deep-rotten stuff to the hospital?

Do you know the government rates?

I know. You took the *contract* knowing full well what the government *rates* were. How is it that Tamli Hospital receives food supplies at the same *rate*? Why does Sadhan Datta not give here? Since you are here no one else took out a *tender* at all.

What are you saying, Gobindo? I undertook this in good faith. You're jerking me around on the doctor's words?

I won't jerk you around. Supply good stuff, Uncle. And don't spread shit about the doctor. He slaves 20 hours. Don't try to remove him.

Jerking around, Gobindo?

I, too, know people at the district town. If a good medicine comes it has to come to you. Whatever the pharmaceuticals give, you take away, is it only a trade? Can one always look for profits?

Listen, I don't try to look out for everything. Okay, I'll check how who gives what.

Gobindo's rough speech bears temporary effect and the raw material for hospital meals becomes minimally normal. But the doctor from the district town doesn't come.

Now Gobindo goes to the district town. He speaks to those whose words the ophthalmologist would value. As a result the doctor says behind his back, Political people are putting pressure. To Gobindo he says up front, I'll go Saturday.

When

By the 9.32 train.

Gobindo thinks he's won a big battle. He passes on the news to the doctor when he returns to the village.

The doctor says, Listen, friend, don't collect another 10 eye patients. Let the old lady be treated.

I will bring her that very day.

This time old Andi comes to the hospital in a new way. Nando carries a pair of scales on his shoulder. He puts a few sacks on one side and his mother on the other. Gobindo walks beside him and puts the scales on his shoulder from time to time.

Reaching the hospital they spread some burlap and lay Andi down under an evergreen. The doctor comes once and wipes off the pus and crust from Andi's eyes. Gobindo and Nando wait.

The day advances. The doctor doesn't come. Gobindo can't think what could have happened. He goes to the railway station. The Station Master says, Why? The doctor has come. That short doctor with the lump on his neck, yes?

Yes. He's come?

Yeah, yeah. Naskar-babu's servant came to get him. He brought a fishing rod, I saw.

Fishing rod!

Yeah. He comes from time to time. Fishes in the pond. I love fishing, too. So I notice. He's come.

By the 9.32?

By the 7.43.

A hundred million *kilocycle* storm rises in Gobindo's brain. Give me your bicycle for a bit, he says.

He rides the bicycle to Hedo Naskar's house. Naskar's servant says, They fishin' in the pond. I jest took food to the masters.

Gobindo goes to the pond-side. A mile-and-a-half away. Hedo Naskar and the doctor have cast their fishing rods in the water in the tree's shade. Nature is calm and lovely all around them. A boy is bathing a water-buffalo at a distance, away from the steps, so that the gentlemen are not disturbed. Whooping-cranes are flying down and up on the water-lilies.

Put aside your fishing rod. Come to the hospital.

Gobindo speaks so loudly that they are both startled.

Hedo Naskar says, He's coming, he's coming! A bit of fishin' . . .

I'll fish him. You'd lose your shit in no time if we did what they did in the old days. Patients are croaking, doctors wasted, and this fucker is fishing. They caught and beat the shit out of you, that's the right medicine. You'd get movin' then.

Coming, coming.

Get up right now. I'll take you on my bicycle. Tie you to a tree. So you either do *private practice* in the district town, or you fish on *call*! A real prince—

Listen, Gobindo . . .

Shut up. I won't let you off easy either, Uncle. You've made a real mistake. If I get angry, I'll make trouble in the area. I won't give a damn for the Patty. Your time for seeing straight has also come.

Gobindo carries the scared and agitated doctor on the rod of his bicycle. His doctoring is breathing its last, he says to the hospital doctor. Sona Doctor's carcass was found on the railway line because he, too, acted this way. Devil's spawn! Here to see a serious patient, he's sucking up to Naskar and fishing in the big pond. He knows Naskar, does he! I'll show him! Our boys are in the district town! Let him step out to go home from the hospital!

The district town doctor now most fearfully promises to examine Andi with great care.

Examine?! He's damn right he'll examine, says Gobindo as he takes off his shirt and fans himself.

Andi is taken inside. After examining her carefully for a long time the district town doctor gradually assumes the role of the responsible doctor and says to the hospital doctor, Operation.

By you?

Yes. You do understand. If I *operate* immediately, that is to say, the *focus* of the *sepsis* . . .

The eye is not gone?

The right eye, maybe . . . all this is *infection*. But if it's not . . .

Here?

Given the situation, we have to do it here.

How

I will go into town and bring everything.

No way, says Gobindo. You are staying here now. My name is Gobindo Das. Write down what you need, I'll bring.

The hospital doctor says, Money—

The district town doctor says, Laddie, I'm coming with you. I'll take stuff from hospital and from my house. I'll also let my family know. So far you can trust me? I'll go with you.

Wait.

Gobindo goes to the Naskar house on the bicycle. Hedo Naskar hasn't got back yet. He says to Naskar's son, Benda, give me 50 rupees. Tell Uncle I asked for it.

Brindaban knows everything. He brings the money without demur. Tell him I'm taking it from the Village Welfare *Fund*, Gobindo says.

Gobindo comes back with the money. Says, Let's go. We'll come back tonight. The train is in an hour and a half.

Can't we come back tomorrow?

No.

At night . . .

Let me light a gas lantern.

Crestfallen, the district doctor accompanies Gobindo. Trouble, big trouble. If a *Party* boy behaves this way . . . he'll buzz off to Calcutta.

At the hospital the doctor says to Andi, Old Mother! I'll admit you now, okay? Have a bite, I'll give you medicine, you'll sleep.

Admittn' me?

Yes.

Old Andi is placed in a dirty bed. Nando brings bread and tea from the railway station and feeds his mother. The doctor gives her medicine and smiling apologetically, says to Nando, Let me wash up and grab a bite. Now that Gobindo has gone, the doctor will surely come, he will surely *operate*, I'll have a lot to do.

Go on, Sir.

Nando now rolls over on the sacking under the tree. Andi's eyes are heavy with sleep. She thinks nothing about the fate of her eyes. She has been admitted to hospital. She will eat all kinds of things at the hospital, the doctor will come again from that district town, Everything jes like a fairy tale one by one! she mutters, amazed, and her face, in sleep within the depths of this fairy tale ravine, looks most fulfilled.